UNDER COVER

UNDER COVER

MaryJanice Davidson

BRAVA

KENSINGTON PUBLISHING CORP.
http://www.kensingtonbooks.com

BRAVA BOOKS are published by

Kensington Publishing Corp.
850 Third Avenue
New York, NY 10022

All Kensington titles, imprints and distributed lines are available at special quantity discounts for bulk purchases for sales promotion, premiums, fund raising, educational or institutional use.

Special book excerpts or customized printings can also be created to fit specific needs. For details, write or phone the office of the Kensington Special Sales Manager: Kensington Publishing Corp., 850 Third Avenue, New York, NY, 10022. Attn. Special Sales Department. Phone: 1-800-221-2647.

Brava and the B logo Reg. U.S. Pat. & TM Off.

ISBN 0-7582-0646-1

First Kensington Trade Paperback Printing: October 2003
10 9 8 7 6 5 4 3 2 1

Printed in the United States of America

For Yvonne Davidson Hemze and Jessica Lorentz Growette.
One a sister by blood, the other by choice.
Either way, I'm doubly blessed.

Acknowledgments

This book would not have been possible without Lori Foster, who, while ridiculously swamped, found time to run a contest and read all the entries. Thanks also to Kate Duffy, who pulled me out of a talented crowd, and the gang at Lori's message board, who never tire of my online babbling. Thanks also to Stacy Sarette and Giselle McKenzie for their unwavering support during a stressful year, and to Karen Williams for generously proofing a rough draft.

Finally, thanks to you, Reader. Without you, none of this is worth doing.

Contents

Author's Note

I love downtown Minneapolis, but not enough to keep from taking liberties. Locals will instantly realize that the Grand Hotel is not, in fact, across from the library, and there isn't a branch of the FDA in Minneapolis. Any other disparities are a result of my overactive imagination, or error. Either way: my bad.

Sweet Strangers

Chapter One

Renee dashed into the middle of the busy street. Leaping like an ungainly brunette gazelle, she managed to avoid death three times before she got to the curb, taking the angry shriek of the bus's airbrakes as a musician takes applause. She didn't slow, but did take time to snatch a look over one shoulder . . . yep. Still about twenty yards behind her. They hadn't gotten a good look at her face.

She darted into the hotel and was momentarily dazzled by the brightly lit chandeliers and the ferocious grin of the concierge. The guy had a hundred teeth. Where to go where to go wheretogo?

She heard the plaintive *ding!* of the elevator, and cruised in that direction. She had to get off the floor. After that . . . well, she'd worry about the rest later. Improvisation was her specialty. The bad news—like she needed more—the elevator was one of those glass cages. Everyone would see her going up.

She saw a few guests amble out, snug and smug in their dark autumn colors, with doubtless nothing more pressing on their minds than where to have dinner. She wanted to choke them and cry on their shoulders at the same time.

As the elevator emptied, a lone businessman walked in, his nose buried in a newspaper. A daring, reckless, and ultimately insane plan popped into her brain and, as usual, was approved by management.

They don't know my face very well; the picture they have is truly terrible, she reminded herself, putting on a burst of speed as the elevator doors started to close. *Plus, they're looking for a woman alone. So . . .*

Renee skidded along the tile and slid into the elevator, almost smashing into the far wall. Darned new shoes; she knew better than to wear unscuffed soles to work. Errr . . . on the run from work.

The businessman blinked at her over his *Wall Street Journal,* then raised his eyebrows as she snatched the paper out of his hands and flung her arms around his neck. "Sorry I'm late!" she panted, then mashed her lips down on his.

This was business, not pleasure. Or was it the other way around? The man was a stone fox, and that was a fact. Thick, wavy brown hair fell almost to his shoulders, an interesting contrast to the so-sober black suit, sky blue oxford shirt, and blue tie with black stripes. She saw that his eyes, in the moment before she sexually assaulted him, were the same blue as his shirt. His hair felt like coarse silk.

Far from shoving her away, or smacking her with his briefcase, the businessman kissed her back enthusiastically and hungrily. She felt her feet leave the ground and realized he'd picked her up, the better to snuggle her into his embrace. Oh, to be snuggled! It had been such a long time. Since—er—what year was it? She wrapped her legs around his waist and let him take her mouth again and again.

Ding!

Sure, she'd been having a rotten day. Week. Month. And yes, the bad guys . . . okay, good guys, *she* was the bad guy . . . were definitely hot on her trail. And she had no money and no place to stay. And if anyone figured out what she'd taken, her life wouldn't be worth spit on a sidewalk. At the very least, she'd never get a job in the industry again.

Ding!

But this man, this amazing man . . . his hands were all over her, big and warm, his mouth was kissing and nibbling, his aftershave smelled like a sunny apple orchard, and—

Ding!

The elevator had stopped.

With deep, *deep* regret, she managed to wrench herself free and put her feet on the floor. It was hard to get a deep breath. All that running, probably. Followed by the finest kiss of her life. Meanwhile, the businessman had thrust his hands in his pockets and was looking her over very carefully. He didn't smile.

"It's all right," he said at last, as she backed out of the elevator.

"What's all right?" She tried not to wheeze. What floor were they on? Who cared?

"Being late. You said, 'Sorry I'm late.' " His voice was a pleasant baritone. His gaze never left her face. To her surprise, he followed her out of the elevator, leaving his briefcase behind. "It's all right."

"Er . . . thanks. Gotta go."

His hand reached out and closed over her elbow. She briefly considered breaking his wrist, then decided against it. She had bigger things to worry about than assaulting Mr. Hottie. Again, anyway.

"Have lunch with me."

"I can't. I have to . . ." *Go. Run. Hide. Figure out what to do with PaceIC. Cry myself to sleep. Jump off a ledge. Kiss you again,* then *jump off a ledge.* "I have to go."

He chuckled, but still he didn't smile. "You misunderstand. I wasn't asking . . . Renee." She nearly fainted as he reached into his pocket and pulled out a badge. "You've got some explaining to do. And you can do it over lunch."

You can do it, dude. First day on the job—shoot, Minneapolis is Hicksville compared to back home. You can do it.

He approached the couple. Mighty cute, both of them, she with reddish brown hair and pretty brown eyes and rosy cheeks, and he with that butch longish dark hair and Paul

Newman eyes. He looked like a million bucks in his suit, but she was way underdressed—leggings, a knockoff purse, and a sweatshirt with the logo "Free Martha."

"Hi, I'm Rod and I'll be your server today."

The woman blinked up at him. "Hi, Rod, I'm here against my will."

"Can I tempt you with the specials? Today we're featuring sautéed sea bass served over a bed of grilled radicchio—"

She set down her water glass, hard. Water slopped over the side and spattered the tablecloth, which made her companion sigh. "Rod, you're not listening. I'm having lunch under duress. This goon here—"

"Oh, now, I object to 'goon,'" the dude with her said mildly. He was pretty blank-faced, but Rod, with the instincts of an experienced waiter, had the strong sense the guy was enjoying himself immensely.

"—assaulted me—"

"Excuse me?" Blue-eyed dude's eyebrows climbed up so high, they nearly dropped off his forehead. "Who assaulted whom?"

"—and dragged me here and is forcing me to eat." The gal finished this absurd tale in triumph, and drained her water glass in three gulps. She belched lightly, which brought another sigh from her date. "Man, all that running made me pretty thirsty. Could I get a refill? Um, like three of them?"

"Right away, ma'am."

"Don't call me ma'am. You're my age, I bet."

He plunged ahead, thinking, *Of course, I'm gonna get the nuts on my first day. It's like a law or something.* "Then we have just a lovely lobster tail which has been brushed with a teriyaki sauce and grilled, which we're serving with wild mushroom risotto."

The woman peered up at him. "You're from New York, aren't you?"

"Yes, ma—uh, yes."

"I recognize the breed," she said to her companion. "Nothing fazes them. I could be on fire and he'd still recite the specials."

True, but I'd hand you a bucket of water while I recited them. "Finally, we have a top sirloin which has been rubbed with pink peppercorns, served with a lovely Bernaise sauce."

"As opposed to a nasty Bernaise sauce?"

"Be nice," her date said coolly.

"Listen, Gestapo Boy, I won't stand for—you know, that last one sounded good, I'll have that."

"I will have the same, but hold the peppercorns," Gestapo Boy said. "And a martini." He looked across the table at the gal and nearly shuddered. "Keep them coming."

"Oh, I like *that*. Who kidnapped who?"

"Whom."

"Right! What?"

Rod was walking away by then, but he heard the dude say a very strange thing. "I can't believe there's a seven-figure price on your head. *Your* head."

"*I* can't believe I didn't knee you in the gonads when I had the chance."

Maybe they were rehearsing a play.

Chapter Two

"So." He sliced off a corner of his steak, forked it into his mouth, chewed, and swallowed. Excellent. "Where is it?"

"I'm not telling you shit," she said with her mouth full, lightly spraying him with breadcrumbs. "As soon as the meal is done, I'm outta here."

"I don't think so."

"I can't believe I kissed you."

"Nor could I. It certainly livened up what had promised to be a dull day. But," he continued cheerfully, "what's done is done. And now we're here."

"*We* aren't anything. I'm having a nice lunch and letting you sit at my table."

"And pick up the check."

"Well, yeah. I can't—" She stopped talking and took a monster-size gulp of her frozen mud slide.

"You can't draw on your bank funds or use your credit cards, because you'll be caught."

She shrugged sullenly.

"Oh, Renee, really. Just give me the vial and this will all be over."

"Ha!"

"What, ha? It will. I could even talk to your boss, Mr.—"

"The Jackal? He won't listen to you. He'd see me hanged if he could."

"Now, that's a bit melodramatic," he said mildly.

"Pal, have *you* been chased the last two days?"

"Ah . . . no."

"Right. Keep your trap shut, then."

"I'd best, or you might stick your tongue into it again."

Her eyes widened and actually bulged, and he had to stomp on the chuckle that wanted to get out, stomp on it and make it gone. If he laughed at her, he could count on getting a face full of frozen mud slide.

"Never mind," he said quickly, hoping to head off the outburst. "Uncalled for and all that. But, Renee, surely you realize you can't keep running and running. Besides, you're not the victim here. You've stolen—"

"*I didn't steal anything!*" Then, startlingly, she burst into tears, put her head down on her plate, and sobbed into her Bernaise sauce.

Within minutes he had settled the bill and brought her up to his suite. She had curled into his side like a weepy shrimp, and he glared at everyone who stared.

Once in the room, he patted her ineffectually until her sobs tapered to hiccups. She felt unbelievably good in his arms, soft where she should be, and lean and defined in other places. Well, she *was* in security. It made sense that she kept in shape. Yes, perfect sense. And she was kind of perfect, too, so lush and sweet-smelling and—

Will you focus, idiot?

"I don't know your name," she said into his collar.

"It's Eric. Eric Axelrod."

"I'm Renee Jardin."

"Yes, I know. You have Bernaise sauce in your hair."

She jerked away from him and her brows rushed together in a glare. "I didn't steal anything."

"So you said. Enlighten me."

"No." She wiped the tears away with her palms. "I need to use the bathroom. Be right out, okay?"

When the door clicked—and locked—behind her, he realized his wallet was gone.

He slammed his hand against the door. "Oh, very nice!" he shouted into the wood. "When did you pick my pocket, you little harridan?"

"I don't know what that is, but it's probably not very nice, so say bye-bye to your driver's license." He heard the toilet flush and ground his teeth. Then, in an outraged squawk, "You work for the National Security Agency?"

Rats. She'd found his old ID. "Not anymore," he said quickly. "As of last week, I am a freelancer. Private eye, and all that."

"Private dick is more like it. And now you're looking for me."

He made a split-second decision and fervently hoped he wouldn't regret it. "No," he lied, "it was just a coincidence. Your company has given your picture to several law enforcement agencies, along with an interesting tale. Apparently you work for bioterrorists—"

An outraged scream: *"What?"*

"—and have stolen something highly unstable and have violent intentions."

He'd heard this absurd tale from Anodyne, and had gotten her file via fax that morning. The NSA couldn't officially become involved—they were codebreakers, not cops—thus he had taken the case. If he turned her in, it would be a tremendous boost to his fledgling career. And if he didn't . . .

Best not to think about that.

He remembered memorizing her file, being struck by her good looks, and thinking that she looked more like Miss Dairy than Miss Terrorist.

It had been the purest—and sweetest!—of coincidences that she had leaped into the elevator and kissed him. What the poor thing hadn't realized was there was a law enforcement convention just down the street, to which he'd flown in for networking. Of course, getting an assignment in the same city as the convention had been pure gravy.

He'd recognized her at once, of course, in that blurred moment before she'd jumped into his arms. The grainy faxed picture didn't do her justice. And it did nothing to showcase her amazing charisma. He could almost see the energy crackling around her when she spoke, moved. Kissed.

Every thought had gone out of his head when those soft, sweet lips met his. And when he'd followed her out of the elevator, he'd nearly staggered. Renee Jardin was an amazing woman, and he was a big believer in love at first sight.

Now, anyway.

When his head cleared, he realized if Renee had gone one more block, she would have been in the middle of five hundred law enforcement officers, most of whom had heard of her. Anodyne was desperate to get her—and her cargo—back. They were spreading their net as widely as they could. So he had instantly stalled her departure with an invitation to lunch. And when she wept, he wanted to leave the table, find her tormentors, and methodically break their fingers.

All this flashed through his mind in half a second. "I really don't work for your boss," he said through the door. "But I would like to help you. I certainly don't blame you for being paranoid, because everyone *is* out to get you. But I'm sure we can discuss this like adults. Won't you come out?"

Silence. Then . . . *flush*.

"Now you're just being childish. If you come out, we can discuss this like rational adults and come up with a plan of action. And—you know, Renee, it's quite difficult to have this conversation with a bathroom door."

Silence.

"Renee? If you come out, I'll buy you another steak."

Silence.

"Renee?"

Blast the woman! He raised a leg and kicked; the flimsy lock broke at once and the door swung open.

Into an empty room.

Chapter Three

Renee chortled to herself as she opened the sliding doors to the deck. What luck that the suite connected to another room—through the bathroom! And what luck that Eric hadn't known. It had been child's play to pick the lock. She'd cut her teeth on bicycle locks as a kid, and this one was only slightly more complicated.

But now what? She couldn't go back down to the lobby. Eric might beat her there. The guy looked like he was in pretty good shape. He sure felt like it, anyway. Worse, she didn't know where the goons had gotten to. For all she knew, they could be waiting in the lobby, too.

If she could get into the skyway system, she could lose everybody. There were skyways throughout downtown Minneapolis, and she could get some distance away and think—for the first time in hours and hours—really think about her position, and what to do, and where to go.

OK. You need to get to the skyway, and you need to do it fast, because Eric isn't going to chat with the bathroom door much longer.

She looked at the street from the suite's balcony. Yup. There it was.

Renee, you're crazy.

"Quiet, inner voice," she muttered. Insanity was the word of the day, and that was for sure.

Silently, she blessed her parents for suggesting she take up gymnastics in addition to karate and aikido, and climbed over the balcony. The skyway was barely fifteen feet down, and only a few feet to the right. She could do this. She was in good shape, and a fall from that height was totally survivable. People did it all the time.

Besides, the alternative was unthinkable.

Eric was gorgeous, Eric was a great kisser, and Eric was the enemy. She wanted to believe in him, trust him, and that made him more dangerous than the Jackal. At least she *knew* the Jackal was bad news. With Eric, she had absolutely no idea. And she was too busy staring at his mouth to be interested in finding out.

Why had he left the National Security Agency? Was it on his own, or had he been bounced? He was awfully young— thirty-six, if his license was right—to retire and go into the Pee Eye biz. What was he doing in town? How had he known her so quickly?

No, best to get clear of him. In particular, his hands and mouth.

She let her hands slide down the bars of the balcony— thank goodness it was fall, instead of winter! She dangled for a moment and screwed up her courage. Then she started to swing her body to build momentum. At the height of her swing, she let go and lunged sideways.

And dropped. And dropped. And hit the roof of the skyway . . . and skidded over the edge. She made a wild clutch and caught the edge of the roof before she plunged over.

"Jesus Christ!"

She looked up, dangling. Her hands were screaming, and her wrists felt like blocks of wood. Eric-the-stalker was staring down at her from the balcony. His eyes were huge.

Well, I'm not going to scream for help like some loser bim. I'll just hang here for a minute and then swing a leg up and be on my way and I'll be just—

"Errrrrrrrrrrrric!"

"Hold on!" he shouted down. Then he disappeared.

The rat bastard! Trust the NSA to disappear when you need them to do something in this *country. So damned typical. So—*

He appeared suddenly, and if she'd blinked she would have missed it. He had obviously backed up to get some room, then bounded up—and over!—the balcony, his momentum carrying him to the skyway. For a moment he was silhouetted against the sky like a suit-wearing bat. Then he landed with a heavy thud, right in the center of the roof.

The bum made it look easy.

Her left hand spasmed and let go, and suddenly her right hand was entirely responsible for keeping her hundred-thirty-two-pound frame attached to the skyway, as opposed to splattered all over Second Street. She shrieked—

—and suddenly his hands were there, locked around her right wrist, and he was crouching in front of her.

She could hardly see him. Stupid wind, it was making her eyes water. As if she didn't have enough problems right now! "Don't let go," she said. "I'll be really really pissed if you do."

"I've got you, sweetheart. But you have to let go of the edge so I can pull you up."

She tried. But it was no use . . . her fingers were spasmed into an unmoving claw. He let go of her with one hand, and gently pried her fingers loose. At least, that's what she assumed he was doing. She couldn't feel his touch. Maybe he was trying to get his wallet back.

After a long moment he stood and lifted her to him as easily as a mother picked up her child.

"You fucking idiot," he said, and hugged her so hard she lost all her breath.

"Whooof! Jeez, let me get my breath."

"I ought to throw you right off this roof. Right. Off."

"Take it easy, you're gonna crack a rib."

"I ought to crack your *skull,* you stupid, stupid girl." He spoke roughly, but gently brushed her hair out of her eyes. "What the hell were you thinking?"

"That it was stuffy in that hotel room and I wanted a breath of fresh air," she said with a straight face, then grinned when he laughed unwittingly.

"Well, Miss Genius, what was your plan for getting off the skyway roof?"

"Well, there are often ladders—"

"Not this time."

"No need to sound so smug," she muttered, then pointed to the large windows of the office building, which connected with the hotel via the skyway. The windows were six feet tall and easily reachable. Plus, it was a Saturday. The building was likely deserted.

"And if an alarm goes off when you break the window?"

"Unlikely, in this neighborhood. If anything's alarmed, it'll be the front door, not the second story window." She looked down as a car honked at them. "Well, that's quite enough attention, I think. I'm outta here. Bye."

"Not without me," he said firmly, and dogged her heels to the window.

"If you come with me, it sort of negates the whole reason why I escaped in the first place," she griped, then broke the window with an elbow strike.

"At least you're wearing a heavy sweater," he said disapprovingly. "As for negating your reasons, I couldn't care less. We have a conversation to finish."

"Yeah, yeah." She reached in, found the catch, turned it, slid the window open, and carefully stepped inside the building, avoiding the broken glass on the floor. She stood for a long moment, listening.

Nothing. No lights, except from the computer screen savers. The rooms were still, that peculiar stillness that comes from an unoccupied floor. The place could be wired for silent alarms, but given the general shabbiness of the cubicles and equipment, she doubted it.

She turned just in time to see Eric step inside. Then he took her into his arms and kissed her so hard she thought her lips would go numb.

"Umm," he said after a long minute.

"Umm? That's it?"

"Strawberry Chap Stick. I love it. Also, you owe me your life."

"Well, I probably would have been able to—"

"You owe me your life," he repeated firmly, and lowered her to the carpet.

Chapter Four

Somehow, her sweater was hanging over the nearby computer monitor, her left shoe was in the cubicle beside them, and her right was over by the coffeemaker. Eric was kissing her mouth, her chin, the soft skin of her throat, and he was giving her goose bumps. Certainly not from the chill in the air; she was far from cold. She was *very* warm, almost too warm, and she pulled and tugged at his clothes until his bare chest was settling against hers.

You don't have time for this.

Shut up, inner voice.

"Stupid back-clasp bra," he growled in her ear, tugging. "Get rid of them. Only front-clasp brassieres from now on."

"Who says "brassieres"? Where the hell are you from?"

"Shut up and kiss me back."

"OK, but after that, I get to boss *you* around."

He laughed into her mouth. She curled up her tongue to meet his; he tasted like martinis and smelled like crisp cotton. She could feel his hands stroking the skin of her belly, then sliding beneath her and fumbling with her bra. There was a wrench—

"Ow!"

"Sorry."

—and then her breasts were free and he instantly captured

one of her nipples with his mouth. He sucked, hard, then eased up and licked, his tongue rasping across the taut flesh until she thought she'd scream.

She clutched double handfuls of his thick, wavy hair, then forced herself to ease her grip and ran her fingers through the silky strands.

"What are you thinking about?" he asked her cleavage.

"That I've never made out with anyone who had long hair and wore business suits."

"And?"

"It's definitely something to write home about," she laughed. Then she gasped as he nuzzled lower, licking the lower curve of her breast. "Oh, jeez, that's *really* great."

"Umm. I was thinking much the same thing. Oh, good—leggings. Easy off." She could feel his hands on her and raised her hips, the better to be stripped. In another few seconds, her pants were hanging over the cubicle wall.

Two days ago she'd been head of security for Anodyne. A day ago she'd been jobless and on the run. This afternoon she was making love with the guy who caught her.

It was madness, but it seemed, oddly, a reasonable reaction to the chaos of the last forty-eight hours. And she was so, so tired of running . . . and he felt so good . . . and held her so gently . . . and his mouth . . . his mouth . . .

She reached down, unzipped his pants, and slowly eased her hand inside. She felt something sinfully soft—silk boxers?—and then grasped his long, hot length. Nothing soft there . . . but still sinful, oh, yes.

He stiffened against her and his eyes rolled up. "Good thing I'm prone," he managed, "because I think my legs just buckled."

This is crazy, crazy, crazy. You haven't even known this guy for two hours.

Shut up, inner—

Well, you haven't!

"Quick," she groaned as she felt him slip a finger past the

elastic edging of her panties. "Tell me something deeply personal."

"Uh—I'm a Capricorn?"

"*Deeply* personal, jackass."

"Do we have to have this conversation while we've got our hands in each other's underpants?"

She smothered a giggle. "Can you think of a better time?"

"Uh—I was born in St. Paul. Joined the Air Force after high school. Used—oh, Christ, that's nice, don't stop doing that—used the—um—GI Bill to—uh—to . . . What was I talking about?"

"Using the GI Bill to pay for college," she replied, delighting in the way he was trembling above her. She was stroking his velvety length, running her fingers up and down, occasionally rubbing the now-slick tip with her thumb. This appeared to be done to good effect, if his harsh breathing was any indication. "Then what?"

"Then I died and went to heaven."

She squeezed, and he groaned. "No, really."

"Um . . . the Air Force paid for my master's in criminal justice. Then the NSA recruited me. Then I got tired of the NSA. Then you kissed me in the elevator and I became your slave."

His fingers were caressing her inner thighs just outside her panties, and his thumb was stroking sweet circles around her tender flesh. She squirmed and spread her legs to give him better access. He bent and nibbled softly on her lower lip, then sucked it into his mouth. She breathed his breath, and it wasn't nearly enough.

"How much longer are you going to make me wait?" she nearly whined. She squeezed again, harder.

"Ah! Don't do that. Never mind, keep doing that. Harder next time. What?"

"What?"

"What did you say?"

"I don't remember. It would be much easier for you to fuck me," she said helpfully, "if you lost the pants and the boxers."

"Thanks for the tip," he said, so dryly that she laughed. "But that's just what I'm afraid of. I—ah—am not in the habit of bringing condoms along on business trips."

"What, are you kidding?"

"No."

Shit. She sighed and threw a forearm over her eyes. *Shit, shit, shit.* "Then you'd better get your hands out of my underpants."

"Well, I was thinking—"

She sat up and shoved him off. "No, no, no. You're right. This was a bad idea. Very very very bad."

"Maybe we could improvise."

"What, Saran Wrap and a rubber band? Pass." She stared at his bare chest. She'd ripped his shirt open a little too roughly; she could see at least two buttons on the carpet. He had the absolute nicest chest. Lightly furred, with yummy tan quarter-sized nipples and amazingly defined abdominals. He really was very—

"—else we can do?"

He sounded so plaintive, she hid a smile. "This was nutty enough without risking my health—or my life. For all I know, you could be riddled with disease."

He snorted.

"I know, I know, but we're not a couple of horny teenagers with no impulse control."

"Funny," he muttered, sitting up and pulling his shirt together. "I sure felt like one five minutes ago. Jesus, how many of my buttons did you eat?"

Teenagers. No, they weren't teenagers. Far from it.

But that gave her a delicious idea. She abruptly straddled him and pushed him back until he was lying on the carpet.

"What now?" he complained, but there was a gleam in his eye she quite liked.

"Well . . . we're pretty charged up . . . and we've decided we're *not* going to be careless . . ." She slid down a bit and began to wriggle against his hips. "But that doesn't mean we have to walk away totally frustrated."

He caught on at once, and put his hands on her ass to pull her closer. She was wearing her panties and her socks, and nothing else. His shirt was open and his shoes were off, but other than that he was fully clothed. So when he pressed her to him and started to twist against her, the friction was absolutely delightful.

"I haven't gotten off like this since I was in college," she giggled, rubbing against him.

"Stop talking now," he growled.

"You'd have to gag me."

"Next time," he promised. He yanked her down to him, holding her shoulders with bruising strength, and then his tongue thrust past her teeth and she groaned into his mouth.

They rocked together; the only sound in the deserted office was their muffled gasps and groans. She felt his hands sliding down, cupping her breasts, forcing them together into deep cleavage, and then his fingers were rubbing her nipples, rolling them between his fingers, pinching them, while he thrust, *writhed*, against her, and she spun away into orgasm, clutching him so tightly she would later notice bruises on his shoulders.

She was drenched, and not just with sweat. She gave not a shit. The only thing that mattered was that amazing feeling, the way her uterus contracted when the waves of pleasure—

"Ah, Eric, that's so good!"

—crashed over her again. And again.

His grip tightened a moment later, very close to pain, and then he relaxed. His forehead was sheened with sweat and he was panting lightly, as if he'd jogged around the block.

"Oh my."

"Exactly."

"That was awesome."

"To put it mildly."

She yawned. "I need a nap. It's been a weird couple of days."

"I need to change my pants."

She giggled. "Gross."

"I'm gross? You're the one who did this to me." He pulled her beside him into a companionable embrace. "I haven't had to—er—change my pants in the middle of the day since I was a teenager."

"I'll bet all the girls were crazy about you."

"Hardly. I was a beanpole, and I stuttered when I got nervous."

"You did not!"

"Swear."

"Huh." She settled against him, got more comfortable. "I figured you for a Big Jerk On Campus type."

"Not until senior year. I shot up six inches and put on thirty pounds of muscle."

"And then?" she teased.

"I had my fair share of dates," he admitted. "But that's quite enough about me. You've got the gift of drawing me out, Miss Renee, but I still don't know a thing about you except that you're a bioterrorist."

"You know that's bullshit," she said, stung.

"Prove it. Tell me about your week. I want to hear everything. Let's go back to my hotel, we'll shower, change—"

"These are the only clothes I have."

"I'll buy you more at the hotel shop."

"You don't have to do that."

"Shit, lounge around naked for all I care. In fact, that's highly preferable. Then you can tell me everything."

"And why would I do that?" she asked, as if she wasn't dying to do exactly that, as if she didn't want to cuddle up with him and let him solve all her problems. Very unlike her! But then, this week wasn't exactly typical. Why not act like someone to be saved, for once in her life? "I've been taking care of myself for a long time. So why should I unload all my troubles on your admittedly broad shoulders?"

"Because I want to help you," he said simply. "And I can, too."

"Oh, is that a fact, now?"

"You watch. By Monday, you could have your life back."

That sounded unbelievably wonderful. In fact, it sounded too good to be true. She thought back to last Monday—six days ago. To be able to go back to that . . .

"And all I have to do is go back to your hotel room and give you the skinny?"

"I'm hoping you'll give me more than that," he said, his gaze dropping to her bare breasts. "Ow! Don't pinch."

"What if more of Anodyne's goons are hanging around?"

He grinned at her. "We can always try your elevator trick again."

They made it back to his suite without incident, for which Renee was profoundly grateful. She didn't think she could handle more confrontations today.

The first thing she did was order room service—she never did get a chance to finish her meal. Then, with Eric's blessing, she called down to the hotel shop and ordered underpants, a T-shirt, and a pair of shorts in her size.

"Tell them to send up a pack of condoms," Eric shouted from the bathroom.

"Forget it!" she yelled back. That was the last thing they needed to get tangled up in—again—and never mind that she was tempted to order a damned case of the things.

"Spoilsport." He walked into the sitting area, a towel draped casually over his hips, his long hair still damp from the shower. She tried not to stare. She failed.

What the hell. He really is gorgeous.

Uh-oh, his lips are moving. He's probably talking to me. "What?"

"I said, shower first, or the skinny?"

"The skinny," she said, "assuming that's not some weird sexual euphemism popular at the NSA." She couldn't help it, she crossed the room and pressed a kiss to his mouth. His grip tightened at once, the towel started to slip, and she reluctantly pulled away and sat on a couch worth more than her entire living room.

She took a deep breath. Why was this so difficult? She hadn't been so reticent about making the guy come, but she couldn't tell him how she'd gone from upstanding citizen to jobless thief. Not too smart.

"Renee?" Eric was adjusting the towel, beneath which there was quite an interesting bulge. "Are you all right?"

"Sure. It's just kind of a long story. The thing is—well, let me tell you how it was . . ."

Chapter Five

Once upon a time, there was a girl named Renee who was never very good at girlie things. When other kids were playing house, she was playing sniper. When other kids were pretending to shoot with their Sega GameBoys, she was in the woods with her father, putting dinner on the table. By the time she graduated from college, she had multiple black belts, deeply enjoyed picking fights with wife beaters, and was interested in finding a job where she could get into fights for a living.

Before she could join the police force, she was recruited by a mean man named Nicholas Jekell, whom many people referred to as the Jackal. Dr. Jekell was starting a company called Anodyne, and he wanted lots of people to protect his company's assets and, therefore, his precious bottom line.

The mean man offered the small-town girl a ridiculous amount of money, and, being up to her eyeballs in school loans, she joined his company, eventually working up to head of security.

Aside from security, there were a great many well-paid, smart people working at Anodyne. One of those smart people was named Dr. Thea Foster, and she was perhaps the cleverest of them all.

Dr. Foster thought up PaceIC, and then set about inventing

it. And once she had invented it and perfected it, she told the mean man it was ready.

And sometime between Foster telling Dr. Jekell it was ready and lunch last Wednesday, PaceIC ended up in Renee's bag.

Renee tried to take it back, only to end up fighting off her own security staff and running for her life.

Renee tried to explain, only to be fired over the phone by Dr. Jekell, who then somehow traced the call and sent other bad men after her.

So Renee ran, but she didn't know where to go. Because Dr. Jekell was so wildly out of control, perhaps there was more to PaceIC than was commonly known. Because Dr. Jekell wouldn't listen and kept sending other mean men after her, perhaps bringing PaceIC back wasn't such a bright idea.

But the question remained: What to do with it? And where to go?

Most of all, why, why, why?

"You don't know how it got into your bag?"

"*No* idea. Shoot, I didn't even know I had it until the shit hit the fan."

"Well, obviously, someone slipped it into your things."

She fluttered her eyelashes. "Oh, Eric, you're so strong and smart! *Thank* you! Because I certainly hadn't figured that out on my own or anything."

He ignored her. "But why?"

"Could you get dressed now?"

"Eh?" Eric ran his hand through his nearly dry hair and blinked at her. "Oh, right. Good idea."

Damned good idea. If he kept prancing around in that silly little towel, she was afraid she'd start to drool.

He absently swung the towel away as he marched into the bedroom, and she had a breath-stopping glimpse of his truly amazing ass—rounded, firm buttocks, skin the color of coffee with lots and lots of cream—did the guy, like, live in a tanning salon?

"Can you think of who would have had access to PaceIC?"

he shouted from the next room. "And who would have a motive to give it to you?"

"Huh? Oh. Right. Um, Thea Foster is the only person I can think of who could check out PaceIC without having to sign a zillion forms and answer a billion questions," she replied, glad he couldn't see she was blushing. *Damn, what a fine ass!* "She's the head of BioSecurity—the money-making division of Anodyne. But she's such a cold fish—why would she give it to *me?* I mean, just to cause trouble? It doesn't make any sense."

Eric walked back in, dressed in dark red boxers—what was it with this guy's silk boxer collection?—and a T-shirt. His hair was loose around his shoulders, and she sat on her hands so she wouldn't get up and run her fingers through it. "Maybe to protect it?"

"Again, that makes no sense. She works for Anodyne, she's making stuff for Anodyne. So why take it away from Anodyne at the last second?"

"It might help us figure out a motive if you tell me what PaceIC is."

"Oh, right. Left that part out, huh? Well, you know how a pacemaker works?"

"Let's pretend I don't."

"Skipped science in school, huh, pretty boy? OK. As even you must know, some people's hearts don't work exactly right. So this guy, John Hopps—"

"Does he work for Anodyne?"

"Uh, no, he died in 1998. He invented the first pacemaker—and a good thing, too, because he ended up needing two of them before he died. Anyway, the pacemaker is a minicomputer that gets implanted in your chest via a surgical procedure, and it regulates your heartbeat with teeny electrical impulses, right?"

"PaceIC," he prompted.

"I'm getting to it, Captain Impatient. So anyway, this invention—arguably one of the most important of the twentieth century—"

"Sure, I see that." Eric was pacing, which was fun to

watch, and slightly less distracting than observing him in a towel. He prowled back and forth in front of one of the suite's three televisions, and added, "Both of my uncles needed pacemakers."

"Hundred and hundreds of thousands of people use them," she nodded. "It's a multibillion-dollar industry. And this really smart gal at work, Dr. Foster—she does *The New York Times* crossword puzzle *in ink,* can you believe it? Anyway, she thought up a way to replace the pacemaker. She developed modified cells that they can inject into the heart. The cells do the job of the pacemaker."

"Say that again. Slower."

"Which. Word. Didn't. You. Understand? Listen, instead of a dangerous operation and a clunky bit of plastic in your chest, imagine a doctor just giving you a shot and poof! Your heart is all fixed. Forever."

He stared at her for a long moment. "Holy shit."

"Right-o."

"Worth a pretty penny, then?"

"About a gazillion of them."

"And what a person-to-be-named planted in your bag—"

"A vial of PaceIC cells."

"Holy shit!"

"You keep saying that." She had to grin. It was great good fun to see him rattled. He was so maddeningly cool most of the time. "But yeah, it's huge. And I've got it. And damned if I know what to do with it."

"And you think this Foster person maybe planted it on you?"

"She's one of two people in the whole company who could do it."

"The other being Dr. Jekell."

"Right."

"But why?"

"Right. What's she up to? If it's even her. If it's not, what's *he* up to? And why is he going batshit trying to get me back? I mean, there's got to be backup info."

"Sure."

"I mean, you can't tell me there's no other trace of Foster's research—notes, computer files . . . hell, the backup server!"

"You're right about all of that. Which makes the question—the *why* question—even more interesting."

"No shit. Is it safe in your bag? The PaceIC stuff?"

"Sure, it can be cool, and it can drop to room temperature. It just can't get hot."

"Are there other vials of PaceIC in the lab?"

She shrugged. "I'm security, not inventory. I mean, I *was* security."

"The reason I'm asking—Foster could always make more, right? So why go after you so hard and so fast?"

"One more time: I have no idea. I'm not brains, I'm muscle. Unless Jekell doesn't want PaceIC to get into the marketplace anytime soon. But that's crazy. He can't make money off it unless people can get it. The FDA is probably going to approve it any day."

"Assuming the FDA even has it."

"Well, sure they do," she said, confused. "They must. The whole company knows they're looking PaceIC over."

"The whole company knows this how?"

"Well, Dr. Jekell—oh."

They sat in silence for a moment, broken when Renee jumped up in response to a knock on the door.

"Calm down," Eric said. "You look like you're about to leap out the window. Again. It's either room service or your clothes." He walked through the door, peeked through the hole, and swung the door wide open. "Lunch is served! Again."

After the waitress had been tipped and left—not without, Renee noticed, flirting with Eric so hard she practically shook his dick instead of his hand—Renee made short work of the hamburger and fries. Eric paced.

"That could get annoying," she commented, watching him.

"Helps me think. You have ketchup on your lip." He stopped pacing, bent down, and kissed it away. "PaceIC, PaceIC . . ."

"Look, I've gotta get a shower." She wiped the burger

grease from her lips—mmmm, rare burgers!—and stood. "I can still smell the Bernaise in my hair. And my clothes aren't here yet. Would you mind getting dressed and running down to see what the holdup is?"

"Sure. Don't go away," he said with mock sternness.

"No worries. Nothing is getting me back into those clothes; I've been wearing them for two days."

"Which reminds me, where have you been sleeping since Wednesday?"

"Who said"—she sighed—"I've been sleeping?"

"Poor baby," he said sympathetically. He dropped a kiss to the top of her head, and went to get dressed.

She snuggled into the complimentary robe—she could get used to suite living—and plopped down in front of one of the televisions. Eric was taking his sweet time getting her clothes. Maybe he was stocking up on condoms. The thought made her laugh out loud.

She could hear the tinny sound of a cell phone ringing, and looked around the room. Eric had left his cell phone on the bedside table, next to his money clip. She dropped his wallet beside the money clip and picked up the phone.

"Hel—" She bent over in a sudden coughing fit—damned throat tickles! They never came along at a convenient time.

"Jesus, Axelrod, you sound like shit. You catch a cold, or what?"

She nearly dropped the phone. Pete Random! She ought to know the voice—she'd hired him. He was a completely unscrupulous private investigator who did all of Anodyne's background checks.

She said, "Mmmph," in as low a grunt as she could manage.

"Listen, when are you dropping off Renee? The boss and I have been waiting all damned day."

"Mmmmph?"

"Shit, we *know* you got her. In your hotel room, no less." An oily snicker. "I mean, jeez. How much time do you need?"

"Mmm-hmmm?"

"Oh, is she right there? Got it. Listen, just get her out to the street. I'll handle the rest. I mean, I know she's into all that chop-socky bullshit, but we can wear her out with sheer numbers. Assuming you haven't already worn her out." She could actually feel Random leering into the receiver, and shuddered all over. "But it's important that you bring the vial, got that? Bring PaceIC, bring the bim, and the boss has a check waiting with your name on it. Tell ya, I *never* seen so many zeros on one check."

"Mmmmmmm."

"And don't be a greedy fuck and hold out for more money," Random snapped. "Jeez, you been on the job—what? A day? And you nabbed her already? You'll get paid."

"Hmmph."

"Right, then. See you in a few."

She slapped the phone shut. Then she gathered up his money clip and wallet and carried them, along with the phone, to the bathroom.

She didn't flush the toilet. Let him fish for them, if he wanted them that badly.

She dressed as quickly as she could with fingers gone numb. Everything was numb. He had lied. Lied and used her and gotten everything out of her. Everything. And she'd believed him. Had let him put his hands on her—had welcomed his hands.

Jekell had hired Eric Axelrod to find her. And so he had. And like a true moron, like some dumbass sitcom heroine, she'd jumped into his arms and forgotten all of her training. All for a pretty face.

She was so furious, her eyes were leaking.

Eric was waiting patiently for the clerk to bag Renee's new clothes when his gaze caught the beautiful nightgown hanging in the far window. He slowly walked over to it.

It really was something, and it was just Renee's color—the dark red would set off her big brown eyes superbly. The long skirt would practically float around her shapely legs. The gown was high-necked, but most of the bodice was made of lace. He stroked the material, pretending Renee was already wearing it, then gave himself a mental shake.

He had to decide what to do, and quickly. Never mind the problem of being in love—and lust!—with someone he'd just met. She was in trouble, and he had to help. He didn't trust that skunk Jekell as far as he could throw him—though since he'd started lifting weights again, he could probably toss the guy pretty far.

Never mind. The money wasn't worth it. Starting his own business with a million dollars—the bounty Jekell had put on her pretty head—wasn't worth it. Renee was an innocent. He believed her story completely, and he had to help her figure out what to do. She needed her life back—and he needed her.

Ridiculous, really. He'd known the woman half a day. But she was so ruthlessly charming, so adorably funny, and so sweet beneath that tough-girl exterior. And so adventurous! When she wasn't jumping out of windows, she was giving him the finest pleasure he'd ever known—and he'd kept most of his clothes on! If he closed his eyes he could see it again: the way she rocked against him, her eyes slitted with pleasure, the way her pale breasts bobbed in front of him, the nipples begging to be sucked—

He gave himself a mental shake. Well. There was more, much more, to Renee than a good fuck. He could easily see himself spending the rest of the life with her, and if that wasn't the miracle of the ages, then what was?

"I'll take this, too," he said abruptly, and the clerk hurried over to lift the gown out of the window.

He'd talk her into spending the night and delay his report to Jekell. In the morning they would see things clearly and would come up with a plan. As long as Random didn't know where they were, things could be delayed at least twelve hours. And he'd order ice cream sundaes from room service. Sundaes with lots of whipped cream. And she'd tease him and call him a pervert and then gasp when he licked all the cream off her—

"Sir? Your purchases?" The clerk handed him the extra bag

and, humming under his breath, Eric walked to the elevators. He had bought quite a few outfits for Renee; who knew when she could safely return home?

Well, that wasn't exactly the truth. He hoped to convince her to come back to Washington with him. She deserved a vacation after the week she'd had. Once they put this whole mess to bed—

Ahhhh, bed. There's a word. Or, more important, a place.

—they could take off somewhere. Anywhere she wanted. For at least two weeks. Possibly longer.

He opened the door with his key card. "Got your clothes, sweetheart," he called out.

Silence. Not even the shower. He felt a tingle of alarm and impatiently dismissed it. She wouldn't. They had agreed. They would stick together and make a plan. She wouldn't just take off. Besides, he'd taken the precaution of having the adjoining door bolted.

Why would she need the other suite when she could just walk out the door?

He ignored the inner taunt and put down the bags. He poked his head in the bathroom and nearly screamed. It looked like someone had been killed in there. His toiletries were scattered and broken, all over the floor. Only his shaving kit had been left alone, but it had been liberally decorated with mouthwash. The toilet was full of—argh! There was his money clip . . . his wallet . . . *and his cell phone!*

Bastard was written on the mirror in shaving cream.

"Oh, shit," he said aloud. What could have happened? Had she found out he'd bought six boxes of condoms? Ribbed for her pleasure? Did—

The phone rang and he jumped for it. "Hello? Renee?"

"Cripes, Axelrod, I'm waitin' all day down here," Pete Random growled. "Where the hell are you two?"

"Pete." Jekell's right-hand sleaze. A nice enough guy, if you didn't mind the fact that he'd break your arm on a bet. "Did you call earlier?"

"What are you, crazy? Like we didn't just talk on your cell

phone twenty minutes ago? You sound a lot better, by the way."

"Twenty minutes ago?" He felt his head spin.

"Look, we're coming in. Get the bim, get your shit, we're going down to Anodyne and finishing this once and for—"

"Stay away from Renee!"

"What the hell's gotten into you?" Random demanded.

"Stay. Away. From her."

He slammed the cell phone shut and galloped out the door. Twenty minutes. And she'd taken the time to trash his bathroom. She couldn't be that far ahead of him.

He had to get to her to explain. More important, he had to get to her before that conscienceless fuck, Random, did.

Chapter Six

Renee watched the street. She had a perfect perch—the library was catercorner from the Grand Hotel. The spanking new building had beautiful windows that were quite tall. She could see what was going on outside, and if she was spotted, she had plenty of time to get gone before they could get to the second floor.

She had spotted Peter Random's car the moment she looked out the window—thank God for back exits and back entrances!—and was waiting to see which direction he went.

Seeing his car gave her a nasty jolt, one almost as bad as the one she got when she talked to him on the phone.

It brought it all home to her. How stupid she had been, and how weak. Her coworker, Laurie, read fifteen romance novels a month, and had once told her there was a phrase readers used to describe heroines who made boneheaded moves.

"T.S.T.L., that's me," she sighed, resting her forehead on the window.

"Too Stupid to Live," the reader in the next row said absently, her nose buried in *Love's Flaming Fury*.

Despite the day—the week!—she'd had, Renee bit back a laugh. Too Stupid to Live was just about right. And, in one of life's weird coincidences, she was standing beside the romance section. "Exactly," she said, and resumed watching.

She saw Eric burst through the doors of the Grand Hotel, almost knocking over the surprised bellhop. Instantly, Random was out of his car and on the sidewalk. The two men squared off like something from the Nature channel, chest to chest and nose to nose, arms waving. It was warm in the library, but despite the temperature, Renee found herself rubbing the goose bumps on her arms.

It wasn't that Peter Random was a blackhearted villain. He just had a conscience of tremendous elasticity. She had argued against his hiring from the moment his application crossed her desk. And had been overruled, for one of the few times in her career, by Dr. Jekell.

"He's got a criminal record," she'd said for the fifth time. She tapped the fax that had just come from Stillwater State Prison. "Multiple counts of assault. The guy can't pass a bar without getting drunk and picking a fight, for God's sake."

"Good," Jekell had replied absently, not even looking up from his P&L sheets. "Then he knows how crooks think."

"He's a snake."

"Mm-hmm."

"He'll do anything if you pay him enough," she added.

"Hey, blondie—"

"I'm not blonde, Dr. Jekell." *If you ever looked anywhere but my boobs,* she remembered thinking, *you'd know that.*

"—I'm sold already. You don't have to keep pitching. Hire him already. And go away."

"You hired *me,*" she said, trying one more time, "to look out for your company's security interests. I don't think giving Peter Random access to all our sensitive material is the way—"

"Bye."

Dismissed. And she'd hired him. And Peter, despite her misgivings, had proven to be a good employee. Scarily good, in fact. No matter whom they needed info on, Random always came up with the goods.

It probably had a lot to do with his appearance. He was huge—close to six-feet-five and probably two hundred fifty pounds, none of it fat. He had thick black hair with just a touch of premature gray, and the cold blue eyes of a German sniper. His fists, when clenched, looked like bowling balls. When he glared at someone, they just about fell over themselves giving him whatever he wanted.

He was smart, too. Worse, he was tenacious—Dr. Jekell's personal pit bull. Once he got his teeth into something, he didn't let go until he was satisfied. Renee thought he was a snake, but she had never denied he had a kind of savage attraction.

It was ironic—she'd been reticent about hiring a convicted felon, and now *she* was the thief, while Peter was the employee of the month.

Knowing Jekell had set Peter on her was upsetting. Knowing Random and Eric were coordinating her capture was terrifying. It really couldn't—

Oh, now, what was this? Random and Eric were having a shoving match—right on Seventh Street! Probably arguing over how best to gift wrap her for Dr. Jekell. And there—yup, Eric threw the first punch, a nice roundhouse, one that probably made the air whistle.

She stared, mouth ajar, as the tussling match became a knockdown, drag-out fight, the kind she usually only saw in bars or at family reunions. The movies made fistfights seem normal, even glamorous. The reality was quite different—it was no joke when the fighters were two men in their prime. People got killed that way.

Shoppers were stopping to rubberneck, but no one was interfering. Wise, because in real life, the person trying to break up the fight usually went straight to the ER.

Random took the punch, staggered back, then recovered with frightening speed and followed up with a knee into Eric's groin.

Eric blocked the strike with his thigh and punched Random in the face again. In another moment, they were rolling all over the sidewalk, fists and feet flailing.

Renee wasn't sure if she should cheer or go down and break

it up before somebody fractured his thick, stupid skull. On the one hand, she loved seeing Eric get smacked around. On the other hand, she hated seeing Eric get smacked around.

No. She'd made enough mistakes today to last a lifetime. Eric was on his own—and if he lost, she wouldn't shed a tear.

The time for gawking out the window had passed. Time to get back to it.

She took the stairs swiftly to the first floor, cornered the first librarian she spotted, and said, "I'm a junkie; I need my fix."

The librarian, a tall, balding man with wispy sand-colored hair, smiled down at her, and his eyes crinkled in a friendly way. "I have that problem myself," he said pleasantly. "Third floor, near the bank of windows on the east side of the building."

A few minutes later, she was logging onto one of the public computers and downloading her e-mail from home. She skipped past the spam—*Refinance your home at zero percent!*—and the porn—*Jenna wants to suck you dry, big boy!*—and slowed to read the ones from work. Maybe someone had some information, some clue, that she could—

Oh. Oh, no.

> *From: Anodyne IT Services (ITSVC@anodyne.net)*
> *To: Renee "Loser" Jardin (Renee45@aol.com)*
> *Date: Wednesday, October 15, 2004*
> *Re: Klepto bitch*
> *Why don't you just give it back, you klepto bitch? It's not yours anyway.*

> *From: Anonymous*
> *To: Renee Jardin*
> *Sent: Wednesday, October 15, 2004*
> *Subject: Just die already*
> *You've got a lot of nerve and if you ask me you should never even show your face around here again*

unless it's to apologize and beg forgiveness. You don't care about anyone but yourself.

From: Anonymous
To: Renee Jardin
Sent: Thursday, October 16, 2004
Subject: Thanks for nothing
    Well, great, I was ready to cash in my options but I guess that won't happen now because YOU'RE A FUCKING THIEF AND I HOPE YOU DROP DEAD.

Renee chewed her lower lip and ignored the impulse to write back and explain to all her detractors. For one thing, there wasn't time. For another, how could she explain when she wasn't sure what had happened herself?

She skimmed past more distressing subject lines—*Choke and die, You're a jerk, The entire IT department hates you, We called the IRS and hope you get audited forever*—absently wondering which one of her so-helpful coworkers had given out her home e-mail address. Human Resources, probably. She'd never known a sneakier bunch . . . they were more rapacious than lionesses.

From: Jennifer Hildebrandt, FDA
To: Renee Jardin
Sent: Friday, October 17, 2004
Subject: Let us help
    Ms. Jardin, you don't know me. I work for the Food and Drug Administration, and we know you're having a rough week. We would really, really like to meet with you whenever it's convenient. Our discretion will be complete, I assure you. Please call me at 612-302-9313, 24/7.
    Sincerely,
    Jennifer Hildebrandt, New Products

Renee stared at the screen. "Good heavens," she practically screamed, "it's the FDA!" As if the security team, Peter Random, the Jackal, and the NSA weren't bad enough!

She knew what that was about, oh yes. They didn't have PaceIC and would love to get it. The question was, what was she going to do about it?

Chapter Seven

The Minneapolis branch of the Food and Drug Administration was, perhaps ironically, located in what used to be a Dairy Queen Brazier just off Lake Street. As soon as she walked through the front door, Renee had to fight the urge to order a Peanut Buster Parfait.

"I'd like to talk to Jennifer Hildebrandt," she told the receptionist, who was sitting at a desk behind the red counter. "And a large chocolate-dipped cone."

The receptionist, who had the cheekbones of an Egyptian queen and looked about a minute past twenty, rolled her eyes. "Thanks. Because I never, ever hear that."

"Sorry. You have to admit, this is kind of a strange place to have an office."

"I admit nothing. Also, we're moving to our new digs next month. D'you have an appointment?"

"No, but she said she'd see me whenever I wanted."

"All right, then." She picked up her receiver, punched a button, and waited a moment. Renee tensed, imagining a team of FDA goons bursting through the drive-thru window and tossing her to the floor. The only thing that happened was that the freezer turned itself off with an audible click.

"Jenn, there's a lady out here to see you." She looked up at Renee and mouthed, "Name?"

"Tell her I'm a lost lamb from Anodyne."

"She says she's a lost lamb from Anodyne . . . uh-huh . . . yeah . . . no, this isn't one of my stupid jokes. Well, that's what she *said*. Hello? Jenn?" She hung up and gave Renee a great big fake smile. "She'll be right out."

The way my week's been going, she'll be carrying handcuffs.

Renee wandered over to the empty freezer and tried to ignore her growling stomach. She hadn't eaten since—when? She had to think about it a moment. Room service in Eric's hotel room. And before that, lunch in the restaurant with the treacherous bum.

Oh, but it hurt to think about that. It hurt more than she would have thought possible. She'd never dreamed a person in good health could be in so much pain.

Quit feeling sorry for yourself. You'll get through this. Eventually.

Yes. Good advice. Great advice, actually, and she meant to take it at once. Enough with the moping. Time to take charge of her life again! Time to—

"Excuse me? Miss?"

She flinched and looked around. "Sorry. You're going to have to speak up if you want to be heard over the voice in my head."

"Good to know," the woman said dryly. She extended a hand. "Jennifer Hildebrandt. And I'm hoping very much that you're Renee Jardin."

"I am. It's nice to meet you."

Hildebrandt was a surprise. Renee had expected a fussy bureaucrat dressed in beetle browns. Big clunky glasses, maybe, and lots of tweed. Hair skinned back in a bun. No makeup, of course.

Instead, Jennifer Hildebrandt looked like an escaped beauty queen. Her hair was long, past her shoulders, and flawlessly blond—the color of a daisy's center. Her skin was so fair it was nearly alabaster, and her coloring was so true to her hair that Renee knew at once that amazing shade of blond was real.

Her eyes were large, expertly made up, and as blue as the sky on a cloudless summer day. Her lips were thin, but they were expertly lined and filled in with a true red that made her skin look paler, and her eyes bluer. She was dressed in blue jeans and a sweater the exact shade of her eyes. Sockless, her white sandals showed off a perfect pedicure.

Thank God I took a shower today, or I just couldn't face this woman. As it is, I feel like Frumpzilla.

"Shall we head back to my office?"

"Uh, sure." Renee couldn't help it; she snapped a look over her shoulder as they went.

"It's all right," Jennifer said, reading her mind. "I didn't tell anyone I wrote you. And since you didn't tell me you were coming . . ."

"People really are out to get me, you know. I'm not paranoid." Just hearing that thought aloud made her giggle. Who was it who said paranoia was perfect awareness? She'd have to look that one up.

Jennifer smiled. "No, you're not paranoid. You'd be surprised at the stories I've heard. And, frankly, I'm dying to hear yours."

"Yeah, it's a real weird tale, all right." She followed Jennifer to a windowless office in the back, and took the proffered seat. "But before I spill my guts—again—maybe you could start with how you knew to even write me."

Jennifer sat behind her desk. "Good enough. Are you familiar with the Food and Drug Administration Modernization Act?"

"Uh, no, I can't say that I am."

"Let's start with that, then."

Oh, goody. A lecture on federal legislation. Renee resisted the impulse to catch up on her sleep as Jennifer began to drone.

"A couple of years ago, Congress amended the original Act, which related to the regulation of food, drugs, bioproducts—things like that, because they knew we'd be facing a whole new ballgame in the twenty-first century. You've probably heard that ninety percent of all major innovations were thought up in the latter half of the twentieth century, right?"

Renee hadn't, but nodded anyway and fought a yawn to a standstill.

"Well, it's true."

"Super."

"If anything, that's understating it a bit."

"Of course."

"And this century is going to be even more amazing than the last," Jennifer went on with scary enthusiasm. "Congress knew, and prepared us for it as best they could."

"That's just fascinating. Really. But, um, what does this have to do with Anodyne?"

Jennifer smiled a gorgeous if-I-become-Miss-America-I-will-fight-hunger smile. "Bear with me. Basically, the new act means the FDA can be a little more proactive. Rather than waiting for a company to come to us—"

"You can snoop."

"A little. Which brings us to you. And PaceIC."

"But how did you guys even find out about it?"

"By law, Anodyne is required to list PaceIC with us before they begin manufacturing. So we knew about it and, as you can imagine, we were very excited to begin the process of getting it regulated and into the marketplace. Can you imagine the possibilities?"

"Yeah, we all—I mean, everyone at Anodyne was pretty excited when Dr. Foster said she was just about finished."

"Right. Just about finished. Then suddenly PaceIC disappeared. Nobody was talking about it, and the paperwork was formally withdrawn from our offices in Maryland. When I followed up, Dr. Jekell claimed they'd run into operational delays and it would be years before PaceIC was ready."

"But that's not—OK, well, I know that's bullshit, because I work there, but how did *you* know it was bullshit?"

The smile dropped off her face and she leaned forward. "I went to school with Thea Foster. She was the only fourteen-year-old in my college sophomore advanced chem class. I also knew about her folks. If she was working on it, I knew the problem wasn't one of design or manufacture. There's just no way. Which meant big trouble for somebody, but I didn't know who. Basically—"

"You smelled a rat."

"Exactly."

"OK, I get all that." Renee shifted her weight and crossed her legs. Damn chairs, they were about as comfortable as sitting in a plastic taco. "But look, I'm still playing catch-up, here. How did you know I had PaceIC? Shoot, I didn't even know right away."

"I'm sorry, that's confidential."

I went to school with Thea Foster.

I'm sorry, that's confidential.

Renee blinked slowly. "Right. Got it. OK. Now what?"

"Now," Eric said from the doorway, "we take this young lady's recommendation on where to bring PaceIC. And then we do it."

Chapter Eight

Thank God! Renee was there, and she was all right! She looked surprised as hell, with her big eyes all wide and pretty, and her big mouth hanging open, but that was all right, he'd explain about the misunderstanding, and she'd understand and forgive—

A walloping pain exploded in his nose and radiated up his face. The room faded away from him in slow, loopy waves as everything went dark. He knew the floor was tile, but hitting it was like falling back onto plush feather pillows.

When he came to, it was to find Renee crouching beside him, pressing a wad of tissues to his gushing nose.

"Wha?" he managed. His head pounded in perfect time with his heartbeat. "Wha?"

"She threw the General Enforcement Regulations manual at you," Hildebrandt said helpfully. She was holding a book the size of a bagel toaster. There was a dark splotch on the binding. "I'm pretty sure she broke your nose. I'll have Tina call an ambulance."

"Doh! Do'd call dee amboolance. Redee, led be eggzz-blain . . ."

"Shut up," she said tightly, pressing harder. "After I get the bleeding stopped, I'm going to kick the shit out of you."

She leaned back to grab fresh Kleenex, and he locked his

hands around her wrists. Startled, she looked down at him. Her lips were pressed so tightly together, they were white.

"I'b *dot* worging with Beter Randob. I bean, I was, bud lader I was jusd drying do keeb hib off you."

"What?"

"'I'm *not* working with Peter Random,'" Hildebrandt translated. "'I mean, I was, but later I was just trying to keep him off you.'"

"Do you mind?" Renee snapped.

"It *is* my office," Hildebrandt replied mildly. "And this is pretty interesting. You think this sort of thing happens every day at the FDA?"

Eric shook her wrists to get her attention again. "Redee, I swear. I'd dever, dever hurt you lige thad. I'd gill byselve first."

Renee glanced helplessly at Hildebrandt, who said, "'Renee, I swear. I'd never, never hurt you like that. I'd kill myself first.'" She cleared her throat. "Um. I think I'll steb—er, step—out a moment." She stepped over him and abruptly shut the door, giving them a modicum of privacy.

"You deserved that book to the schnozz." Renee wrenched her wrists free, grabbed more tissues, and pressed them against his nose and mouth. "You're lucky I didn't fracture your damned skull. The only reason I'm even taking care of you is because I don't want you to sue me for assault." Her mouth turned down bitterly. "Or turn me over to one of your cop buddies. Or Dr. Jekell."

"Never," he said. He felt his nose tentatively. The bleeding had stopped. He grabbed the sodden Kleenex and tossed them toward Hildebrandt's wastebasket. "Oh, never, Renee."

"Shut up. I've got to get your nosebleed stopped."

"It's stopped. Also, I'm in love with you."

Now her lips were trembling. Funny how it tweaked his heart to see her grim expression falter. Her great dark eyes brimmed with tears as she said, perfectly calmly, "What a liar you are."

"Not about this. I should have told you the truth, but I was afraid you'd run again."

"You didn't tell me, and I ran. Again." One lone tear spilled down her cheek, and then her gaze hardened. "And why are we having a conversation? I'm not speaking to you."

He grinned, even though it hurt a little. He could feel the tissues around his nose and mouth beginning to swell. "Could have fooled me." He reached up and thumbed her tear away. "Don't cry, babe. I can handle anything but that. Even the way you suck at not speaking to me."

Renee looked around for another book, but before she could get up, he pulled her down and kissed her. It hurt, but he didn't give a damn.

She wrenched away, but he saw with satisfaction that her eyes were bright and she was panting a little. "Quit that."

"I decline."

"There's plenty more bones I can break."

"Worth it."

"You crumb." She put a hand over her eyes for a moment and he heard her take a deep breath. "How could you do that?"

"I didn't do anything," he said patiently. "I had plenty of opportunities to turn you over to Random, and I didn't take them."

"Liar."

"No, and I can prove it." He slowly got to his feet. The room tilted to the left, tilted to the right, and then steadied. His stomach heaved, then settled. "Do you *see* Peter Random anywhere?"

She stared up at him. "Well . . . why didn't you? Turn me in, I mean."

"Partly because I felt sorry for you. But mostly because you're a helluva kisser. I unofficially resigned the moment you sexually assaulted me in the elevator. I just hadn't gotten around to telling Anodyne yet."

"Then that fight I saw . . ." His heart lifted as she giggled. "That was you and Peter fighting over—"

"Let's just say Random didn't accept my resignation." Remembering the street-side tussle, he grimaced. "Guy's got a punch like a bulldozer."

"Poor baby."

"And he fights dirty, too! Kicked me right in the—never mind. Suffice it to say I nearly lost my lunch right there in the street in front of all those people."

"Awwwww."

"Look." He showed her his knuckles, which had been scraped raw. "Random kept hitting me over and over with his face."

She laughed and kissed his knuckles. He felt like doing a cartwheel, sore 'nads and all. "So I'm forgiven?"

"On a trial basis. But when you're feeling better, we're going to have a serious talk on why it's not nice to deceive women with good aim."

"Actually, I figured that out all on my own." He gingerly felt his swollen nose.

Jennifer poked her head into the office. "Everything settled, then?"

"For now."

Jennifer walked in and sat down behind her desk. "Well." She smiled up at Eric and extended a delicate paw. The nails were long, spade-shaped, and pearly pink. "I don't believe we've met."

"Eric Axelrod."

"Jennifer Hildebrandt. How in the world did you know where to find Renee?"

"Good question," Renee said. "I can't believe I didn't think of it."

"Long day?" Jennifer suggested.

"Long week. Well, Eric? Did you bug my—ohhhhh, wait."

He started to sidle toward the door. "Now, Renee. I only did it because I have your best interests at heart."

"Stop trying to wriggle away, coward. Stand there and take my wrath like a man. You figured out a way to download my e-mail from the Web, didn't you?"

Jennifer's brows arched. "A neat trick."

"He used to be a spook," Renee explained.

"Please," he said, offended. "We prefer the term Super Studly Spies."

"So after you and Peter bumped fists, you took off for your hotel room, hooked up your laptop—"

"Thankfully, it was the one piece of my equipment that escaped your fury."

"Only because I didn't see it, buster. Then you used one of your spook pals to get into my e-mail, found Jennifer's message, and came here, figuring I'd do the same. I'm just glad Pete Random didn't think of it, too."

"He's at the ER, getting stitches." Eric inclined his head modestly, then jerked it back as she made a sudden move toward his face.

"Easy, pal," she said, sounding amused. "I was going to hand you this." She pressed a fresh Kleenex into his hand. "You're kind of disgusting right now, with all that dried blood all over your face."

"Oh, I don't know," Hildebrandt murmured.

Renee glared at her. "So what now?"

"A fine question. Do you have PaceIC on your person?"

"No, but it's somewhere safe."

"You left it somewhere?" he practically yelped.

"I didn't know what kind of situation I was walking into here," Renee explained. "For all I knew, Jennifer's e-mail was a fake."

"True enough," Jennifer acknowledged. "But PaceIC is somewhere accessible?"

"Sure."

"Well," Jennifer said, "you've got a decision to make. You can destroy it, and Dr. Jekell will have no reason to keep chasing you."

"And presumably, Dr. Foster can make more," Renee added.

"Correct. Or you can take it back to Anodyne. Or you can take it to another biotech firm."

Renee hesitated. "I don't know about that. I mean, we

know Jekell's up to no good, but to take company property and give it to another . . . that's pretty rotten."

"I guess that depends on your definition of rotten."

Eric raised an eyebrow. "Do tell."

Jennifer stood, and began to pace behind her desk. Since there was only about four square feet behind her, the effect was claustrophobic on her audience, to say the least. "What's Dr. Jekell's motivation? That's the question on everyone's mind. So how best to find out?"

"Uh . . ." Eric crumpled up the Kleenex and tossed it in the wastebasket. "Ask him?"

"I must have hit you a lot harder than I thought," Renee said kindly. "Either that, or you never met the guy. He won't tell us shit. You could stick your gun in his ear, and he wouldn't tell us shit. What about your e-mail trick? Can you do the same with Jekell's work e-mail?"

"You think he's dumb enough to e-mail his plans back and forth on Anodyne's server?"

"Not dumb enough. Arrogant enough. He's told lies about me and he's got half the world chasing me. What's a little indiscretion on top of that?"

"Good point," he admitted. "But the thing is, downloading your stuff was a one-time-only favor. I can't play that card again."

"Why not?" Renee asked.

"Let's just say I saved the life of a higher-up. And I had one favor to call in because of that. Well, I cashed the chip."

"To find me?"

"Sure." Besides, he'd probably save the life of another member of the royal family one of these days, get another favor. And even if he didn't—well, it was worth it.

Renee squeezed his hand affectionately. Unfortunately, it was his bruised hand, and he tried not to yelp. "Well," she said thoughtfully, "I suppose we could go into the belly of the beast."

"You mean Anodyne?"

"No, my grandma's house. Of course Anodyne. Try to find

out what Jekell's motive is, and figure out what to do with PaceIC from there."

"I heard none of this," Jennifer informed them. "No indeed. Breaking and entering and violating privacy? I work for the FDA, not the FBI."

"Then we'll take our illicit chitchat elsewhere," Renee said haughtily.

"Please. And, Renee—should you decide Anodyne is *not* the place for PaceIC, do give me a call. There are several local manufacturers who would love to crank it out into the market."

"How would they even know about it?" Renee asked.

"Freedom of Information Act?" Eric guessed.

"That," Hildebrandt said, "and the fact that I'm a terrible gossip. Jekell burned a lot of bridges, and he's trampled a lot of careers. Plenty of people in this business are itching for some payback."

She said it so coldly, Eric and Renee glanced at each other, a little alarmed.

"Jeez," Renee said, sounding impressed.

"Don't fuck with government bureaucrats," Hildebrandt said solemnly. "We'll tear out your spleen and eat it in front of you."

Chapter Nine

"This is nuts," Renee muttered.

"Pretty much, yes."

"We're going to get caught."

"Doubtful. And even if we are, it'll be harder for Jekell and his evil minions to disappear both of us."

They were hiding under a conference table on the executive level, second floor, east wing. Jekell's office was six doors down. Renee's access card no longer worked, of course, but she knew all the building's weak points, and the timing of the security sweeps. Breaking in had been fairly simple. And at this hour—early evening—there were few people in the building. The cleanup crew, and some lab personnel. Certainly none of the executives worked much past five o'clock.

They were listening to the hmmm-*whoop* of the cleanup crew vacuuming the suite. The crew was in Jekell's office now, and once they left . . .

"Just think," Eric whispered in her ear. "This time tomorrow you could have your life back."

"Doubtful."

He propped himself up on an elbow and looked at her. "Why?"

"You think Jekell's going to say, 'Just kidding!' and give me my job back? Either way, I'm out of work, and I can forget about any kind of reference. Plus, he's spread lies about me all over the place. Tough to undo that. I'll never work in biotech again, that's for sure."

"If we can figure out what he's up to and get the story out . . . well, this *is* the decade of the whistleblower. Maybe you'll get your picture on the cover of *Time* magazine."

"Maybe I'd just as soon eat my own vomit."

"Publicity shy, eh? Well, I bet Jennifer Hildebrandt could help you out."

"Ugh. No thanks. I mean, she's nice and all, but I'd just as soon not be known as 'the funny one.' "

"What are you talking about?"

"Oh, come on. Did Random punch you in both eyes? She's about the prettiest woman I've ever seen."

"Oh." Her eyes had adjusted to the near dark, and she could see him frown. "I guess so. If you like that type."

"The gorgeous, thin blond type with great knockers," she said dryly. "Don't tell me you didn't notice."

"Renee, I was worried about you. Hildebrandt could have been a six-hundred-pound iguana for all I cared."

She stared at him. He sounded serious. He *looked* serious. Was he really so into her that he didn't notice a beauty queen, not even when she was right under his nose?

"Besides," he continued, "if nothing else, you can come and work for me."

"Oh, really?"

"Mm-hmm. Of course, constant nudity would be a given. I'd stick it—"

"Careful."

"—in the first line of your job description."

She rolled her eyes, but before she could retort, he had pulled her toward him and wrapped his arms around her. He kissed the top of her head and murmured, "I was very worried about you this afternoon."

"You deserved to be." She tried to sound tough and uncompromising—sort of a Drew-Barrymore-during-the-married-to-Tom-Green-years tone—but he smelled great. And his arms around her felt so good. She could go to sleep in these arms. Ah, sleep . . . how good would that be? Just to snuggle up to this man and doze off knowing everything was all right, knowing she was safe. "How d'you think I felt, hearing that Random was waiting for me right outside your hotel?"

"I'm sorry," he said soberly. He dropped a kiss to her brow. She could still hear the crew vacuuming; it was a faraway drone and, tired as she was, weirdly soothing. "I should have told you the truth right away. I was afraid. A stupid, stupid mistake."

"Also, you look like a monkey and you smell like one, too."

"Let's not get carried away." Now he was trailing kisses down her face and nuzzling into the hollow of her throat. "Ummm . . . what's that you've got on?"

"*Eau de* Fugitive," she said dryly, then gasped laughter as he nuzzled a ticklish spot. "Quit it! This is neither the time nor—"

"Actually, it's the perfect time; we're just sitting here—well, lying here—waiting. And as for places, I could think of worse ones than on the warm, carpeted floor of an empty conference room."

"You're still on probation, pal."

"Let me see if I can get on the parole officer's good side." He tugged on her shirt and she heard the *pting! pting!* of the snaps parting. He sucked in an appreciative breath when he realized she hadn't bothered with the bra this afternoon.

"I didn't have time for underpants, either," she said, reading his mind. She grinned when he groaned. "Hey, time was of the essence. I had to beat feet out of there—I figured you were running upstairs with Random and his goons."

"Please stop talking about Peter Random while I'm trying to seduce you."

"Why? He's so tall, so strong, so—er—hairy." She sucked in a breath as he tongued her nipple. "I'd like to protest again for the record, but, frankly, if you stop doing that, I'll toss another hook in your face."

"I hear and obey." His tongue was rasping across the sensitive flesh of her nipples, pausing occasionally to suckle and dart and jab, and then he was kissing her cleavage. "God, you smell like wild roses."

"I think that's hotel soap."

He groaned again, the sound muffled against her flesh. "You're killing me."

"How *is* your nose, by the way?"

"Who cares?"

"Tell you what," she said, wriggling against him, rapidly unbuttoning his shirt and squirming out of her own, "I'll stop with the one liners if you shut up and fuck me. I assume you brought condoms this time?"

"Why yes, I did! They're still in my pocket from when I went downstairs to get your clothes."

She felt him, her fingers deftly slipping into his pockets. "Jeez. Are those six boxes of condoms in your pockets, or are you just happy to see me?"

He was laughing and struggling out of his clothes while she kissed and bit and licked everywhere she could reach, and they wrestled together while shushing each other. In moments, they were nude and sliding against each other as if they'd been intimate partners for years. In their haste, they tore through the first two condoms they tried to open.

"Calm down," Eric said, still laughing, "you're going to wreck them all."

"*You* calm down. Stupid foil thingies—ah!" She pulled one, intact, from its packet and gently rolled it on, savoring his throbbing length. "Hey, neat. Ribbed for my pleasure."

"I live to serve."

One ear cocked for the vacuum cleaner, she crossed her ankles behind his back as he surged forward. Just touching him was a pure pleasure; he was lithe and muscular, with the broad shoulders of a swimmer. Her hands slipped and slid all over him, groping; she could never, ever touch him enough.

She knew she was ready and he knew it as well. There was no need for anything more, not even words. She arched to meet him as he parted her with his fingers and pushed inside. It was like being entered by an ideal, a dream—a dream hung like a stallion, frankly; she could practically feel him in her throat. He slid and pushed and thrust and she tightened her grip, arched her back to meet him, and for a long while there was only their harsh breathing, the sound their stomachs made, clapping together, and the *vrrrrrr-mmmmmmmm* of the vacuum six doors down.

His hands were in fists on either side of her head and he was panting, groaning, into her neck. They fit perfectly. It was really quite miraculous.

She slid her hands over his shoulders, down his back, over his taut buttocks, marveling at the feel of him, the smell of him, the way he was nearly helpless in her embrace, so intent on having her he'd blocked out everything else. She realized he was whispering her name over and over as he pushed inside her again and again.

She could feel the muscles flexing in his butt as he worked over her, could see the sheen of sweat on his forehead, and over all that, more wonderful than all that, he was still whispering her name.

Renee gently bit his earlobe, and sighed when he shuddered above her. He pulled back, then licked her lower lip and slipped his tongue into her mouth. At the same time, he put his hands on her thighs, spread her apart, and then stroked her clit with his thumb while just below, his cock reared and plunged and took.

The sudden sensation swamped her and she would have screamed, but his mouth was bruising now, possessing, taking, and the only sound that escaped was a muffled moan. And still he stroked and teased until she was shaking, until she was coming, until she saw dark stars exploding before her eyes, until he stiffened above her and stopped breathing for a long moment.

"Oh."

"That's it? Oh?"

"How about, oh, God, put it in me again?"

He chuckled in her ear. They were lying on their sides on the carpet, curled up like spoons in a drawer. "I think I'm going to need a few minutes."

"That's all right, I think I'm going to need a day and a half." She sighed and nuzzled the hairs on his forearm. "What a week."

"Say you love me," he ordered.

"Babe, I don't even *know* you."

"Well, I don't know you, but I'm so in love with you I'm sick with it."

"That's flattering. Can we compromise and say I love your dick?"

"You have no soul," he grumbled.

"Eric, can I ask you something?"

"Of course."

"Why'd you leave the NSA?"

He was silent for a long moment, and then replied, "To be honest, I didn't want to be a codebreaker or a codemaker anymore. This is going to sound dumb—"

"I'm not surprised," she interrupted, hoping for a smile.

"Ho-ho. Well, a couple months ago, my neighbor's husband turned up missing. And she was going out of her mind trying to find him. She was upset, the kids were upset, the guy's boss was calling every other day—a real mess. The cops weren't much help—DC is a big place, with a lot of problems.

"So I felt sorry for her and did some digging, and it turned out her husband had been mugged, had his wallet stolen, then been in a car accident. He was OK, but he had his brains rattled pretty good and the hospital didn't have any ID. Anyway, long story short, I found him. And—well, it was just really satisfying. Reuniting them. I know that working for the NSA means being part of a bigger purpose, but I don't see anything wrong with being part of a smaller purpose. Not if you can help out a nice lady once in a while. That's all."

"Huh. Well, good for you. A lot of people are stuck in jobs they hate. And they never, never change, because inertia is easier."

"Yes, not everyone is lucky enough to be framed for theft and then fired," he said cheerfully. "To be continued, hopefully in a proper bed later this evening. I don't hear the vacuum anymore."

She started guiltily. Jesus! For a moment—well, for about fifteen minutes—she'd forgotten why they were there. She really *was* getting Too Stupid to Live.

They dressed in the darkened room and climbed out from under the table, but before she could get to her feet he grabbed her and kissed her on the mouth, a hearty smack. "Say it," he ordered.

"I love your dick," she replied obediently.

He sighed and released her. "We'll talk later."

"About your dick?" she asked brightly.

"You're killing me, Renee . . ." He stepped to the door, but before he could open it, someone in the hall did it for him.

Chapter Ten

Renee would have shouted in surprise, but for the hand Eric clapped over her mouth. So what escaped was, "Gmmph!"

An extraordinarily tall woman was framed in the doorway. She would have been striking in stocking feet, but her pumps and the hair piled on top of her head made her easily over six feet. She was wearing a white lab coat that fell past her knees, cat's-eyeglasses, and a gold pin of some sort on her left lapel.

Gold pin . . . wait just a minute.

"Dr. Foster!" Except Eric was still muffling her with his hand, so what came out was, "Dgguh Uzzuh!"

"Renee," the other woman said, and nodded.

Eric slowly let go of her mouth, then grabbed her hand and tucked it into the crook of his elbow. "Uh . . . we were just . . ."

Dr. Foster's assessing gaze missed nothing. Renee fought the urge to shuffle her feet and duck her head. She could just imagine what Dr. Foster was seeing: They were mussed, disheveled, and reeked of sex. And to be caught by IQ, of all people! The original Ice Queen!

"Really, Renee."

"Uh . . ." She fell back on her trademark statement. "It's been a crazy week?"

"What in the world are you doing back here? Tell me you didn't come here to return PaccIC."

"Uh . . ."

"And after all the trouble I went to," Dr. Foster scolded, folding her arms across her chest and looking not unlike a stern schoolteacher. "Disabling the security sensors and slipping it into your bag and telling Dr. Jekell you used your security access to steal it. Then you bring it *back?*"

"Oh, here we go," Eric muttered. He tightened his grip on her hand. Good thing, too, because she was suddenly in a punching mood.

"I don't care if you *are* bigger than me," Renee snapped. "I'm kicking your ass all over this conference room! D'you have any idea what you've put me through?"

"Irrelevant."

"*What?*"

"Oh, sorry," Dr. Foster said coolly. "Irrelevant means unimportant, or immaterial. It's—"

"I *know* what it means, IQ!"

"Maybe you could help us out," Eric panted, restraining Renee with difficulty. "We're trying to figure out why your boss has gone completely crazy over PaceIC."

"Ah, so that's why you're here. And I just thought you were looking for a convenient place to couple."

"Our coupling is none of your damned business!"

Dr. Foster stepped back to avoid Renee's kick. "It is when you do it in the corporate boardroom. I swear, I will never understand why people who are reasonably intelligent . . . never mind."

"Did you hear that?" Renee said to Eric. "She called us reasonably intelligent!" She pretended to wipe away a tear. "So touching . . . but I promised myself I wouldn't cry . . ."

"Enough facetiousness."

"I have no idea what you just said," Renee admitted.

"If you're thinking you'll break into Dr. Jekell's office and crack open his laptop, you'll never get into the system, not with all the upgrades he's forced on us in the last seventy-two hours. Consider yourself lucky I happened to see you on the monitors before anyone else."

"How could you—"

"I have a feed into my computer station in the lab," she explained. "It runs five minutes ahead of the feed Security gets."

"You bitch!"

Foster didn't blink. "If you're going to work for a sociopath, it pays to have information before he does. Count your blessings I came ahead to warn you. Now please leave, and be sure to take PaceIC with you."

Renee restrained herself from saying, "Nyah, nyah, we didn't bring it, so there!" Instead, she glowered at IQ and worked on prying Eric's fingers from her elbow.

"Why?" Eric asked.

Foster had already turned to leave, but now she paused and turned back. "He doesn't want to sell it," she explained, pushing her glasses farther up onto her nose. "Didn't you know? The biggest pacemaker manufacturer in the world is in China, and they made him an offer he couldn't refuse. Bury PaceIC, let them make the clunky mechanical pacemakers for another ten years, and they'd make it worth his while."

Renee practically heard the *click* as everything—finally—fell into place. "So for a pretty penny he keeps the lid on PaceIC?"

"Six billion."

"Damn!" she and Eric said in unison.

"Per year."

"That sneaky son of a bitch." Eric wasn't entirely able to keep the grudging admiration out of his tone. It wasn't lost on Dr. Foster, who fixed them both with a freezing glare.

"I didn't work eighty-hour weeks for six years so that conscienceless bastard could hide my invention from the public. So people who can be cured with a single injection must suffer through an invasive operation that doesn't always work. So the Jackal can make *money*."

Yikes. Renee refrained herself from taking a step back. Foster—the Ice Queen herself!—looked like she was going to spontaneously combust. Her glasses had slid down her nose again, and she batted them back up in a quick, savage gesture. Her hand, Renee saw, was trembling.

She had nice hands, for a lab geek. Long, with the thin tapering fingers of a pianist or surgeon. And why would those shaking fingers make her think of the personnel files in Security? Sure, she read everyone's files when they were hired, and read them again when she had Random run background checks on them, but why was she thinking about that now?

She was the only fourteen-year-old in my college sophomore advanced chem class.

Sure, Foster was a genius, everyone knew that, but why couldn't she get the mental image of Dr. Foster's personnel folder out of her head?

I also knew about her folks.

"Dr. Foster. Didn't I read somewhere that your folks died of heart failure? Both of them? Like, within a year of each other?"

Instantly, Foster was calm again, almost glacial. The transformation was startling to watch, and Renee felt Eric take her hand again. This time, she let him. She even squeezed back.

Dr. Foster smoothed her hair back with her palms, then stuffed her hands in the pockets of her lab coat. "It doesn't matter now," she said, perfectly calm. "If you don't mind some advice, Renee—"

"Advice from the woman who turned my life into a train wreck? Sure, bring it on."

"—take PaceIC to my friend Jennifer."

"Turn it over to the FDA?"

"No, to Jennifer, who happens to work for the FDA. She's actually quite a good scientist. She has the skills to reverse engineer it and see that an appropriate company—ah—finds it and puts out their own version within the year. Anodyne can still make plenty of money off it, they just won't be able to hide it for a decade."

"Well . . . that seems like a good plan, but . . . why me? Why didn't you take care of this yourself? Why wreck *my* life?"

"It doesn't seem terribly wrecked," she said, looking Eric up and down.

Renee ground her teeth. "Well, why not go work some-where else? Why destroy my reputation just to stay here?"

"Better yours than mine," she sniffed. "And I still need Jekell's trust. I have more work to do here."

She neatly sidestepped Renee's crescent kick. "You don't have time for this nonsense," she added emotionlessly. "They're here."

Renee stopped in mid windup, just as Eric grabbed her elbow. "Argh, you're cutting off the circulation. Ease up."

"Did you say they're *here?*"

Renee looked up at him. "After you had that fight with Random, when he knew you weren't going to help him, you went back to your hotel room."

"Sure, I had to. Because—"

"Giving Random plenty of time to put a tracer on your rental car. He'd know what it looked like; he probably met you at the airport."

"Well, yeah, but come on. You're saying he just drives around with a box full of tracers, so anytime he wants he can just—oh, shit, of course he does, he works for the Prince of Darkness. Shit. *Shit!*"

"Enthralling. But ultimately boring. Good luck," Dr. Foster said, and walked out.

"Christ," Eric said, shutting the door behind her and hur-rying to the window. "That's the most terrifying person I've ever met."

"And she's on *our* side. I think. Remind me to track her down and wring her neck later. Stupid, stupid! I should have realized Random would have a way to keep track of you. God, where is my head this week?"

"Don't be so hard on yourself," Eric said, peeking through the blinds. "You've been distracted. Falling in love will do that."

She snorted. "Sure. That's exactly what the problem is. Me, I'm starting to think I deserved to get bounced from Security."

"Oh, quit it. I had ten years with the NSA and it never occurred to me to put a bugkiller in the rental car, so don't feel bad."

"Actually, that does cheer me up a bit. But now what, ace? I mean, no way am I giving PaceIC back now. Which is probably something I shouldn't share with Peter or Dr. Jekell."

"No shit. What's the quickest way out of here?'

"The front door."

"Besides that."

"Well . . . we *are* only two stories up . . ."

"Forget it. I'm done with stunts for the day."

"There's a private elevator in Dr. Jekell's office; it dumps us off in the back and we could slip out that way."

"Fine." He grabbed her hand and ran out the door and down the hallway. She noticed for the first time that he had buttoned his shirt wrong, and put a hand over her mouth to hide the grin.

"What a day," he groaned.

"Welcome to my world."

"What kind of locks do you have on these offices?"

She jogged beside him. Hand in hand! Aww, it was so romantic. If she wasn't a nervous wreck about Random practically breathing down her neck, she might have taken a minute to appreciate the situation.

But now that she knew what was at stake—the cardiac health of zillions of people!—she felt like she would vomit very soon. Possibly within the next two minutes. It had been confusing, but less frightening, when she just thought Jekell took her for an ordinary thief.

"Renee?"

"Sorry—um, just standard locks. It's a lot harder to get into the files and the computers than just the doors."

"Good. Here." He gently pushed her against the wall, out of the way, then raised a leg and kicked, hard, just below the doorknob. "Ow!"

"Probably should have put your shoes back on after we had sex," she suggested helpfully.

"I think I just broke my foot."

Don't laugh. It probably hurts like hell. Don't you dare laugh.

She cleared her throat. "Here, stand back, I'll take care of it."

"Like Hell. I'm a modern man, but even I've got my pride." He stared down at his bare feet. "All right, we'll do it together, on three. One . . . two . . . *three!*"

The door flew inward with a satisfying crash and they jumped inside. Renee turned just in time to see Peter Random running straight toward them, and the short, bulky form of Dr. Jekell was right behind him.

She slammed the door shut, but of course it wouldn't lock.

"The elevator is behind that door, there; it looks like a coat closet. Foster was right, here they come!"

Eric wrenched open the door, already reaching for the buttons, and saw the elevator doors.

Along with the OUT OF ORDER sign taped across them.

Chapter Eleven

"Shit!"

"You say that a lot," she commented.

"Actually, I don't. Just today, I guess. What kind of a top executive doesn't get his personal elevator fixed?"

"The cheap kind."

He spun away from the doors and got behind Jekell's desk. He set his weight and began to push it across the carpet. Renee was impressed; the thing was mahogany and weighed as much as a Volkswagen. She moved out of the way just as he slid it against the door, which promptly rattled in its frame.

"Cough it up, you bitch!" Dr. Jekell.

"Come on, Renee, quit jerking us off." Random.

"It's nice to be popular," she commented.

"Assholes," Eric muttered. He was walking in a tight circle and she noticed the way his gaze flicked from one spot to another—door, door, window, bathroom door, ego wall, picture frames, window. Assessing targets. It was kind of sexy, if nerve-racking. She was pretty sure he hadn't been doing that while they were horizontal in the conference room, but there was no way to—"Thank God you ran into me today."

"Oh, I was *just* thinking that," she said sarcastically. She flinched as the door rattled in its frame again. Jekell was short, but built like a fire hydrant and about as thickheaded. She had no doubt he'd get the door open in the next few minutes, especially with Peter Random's help. "Let's blow this joint, what do you say?"

"Working on it," he muttered.

She crossed the room, jerked up the shades, and pointed. "Look. That building? It's the custodian's storehouse."

Eric came swiftly to her side and looked down at the small, square building on the ground. "What is that, about a ten-foot drop?"

"Yeah. Then we can get to the ground from that roof, and hotfoot it to the car. It'll hurt, but we probably won't break anything." She shoved the window, but it only popped out about six inches.

"Renee, *let us in right now, you fucking bitch!*"

She flinched. She couldn't help it. In her entire life, no one had ever spoken to her like that, in a tone of such venomous hatred. Certainly no one she'd ever worked for.

Eric was looking at her with some concern, and she forced a smile. "Kind of sounds like my grandpa before we put him in the home."

"Uh-huh. Stand back." He picked up the desk chair and, when she stepped away, swung it into the window, which shattered with a satisfying crash. He pulled off his suit jacket, which made his misbuttoned clothing and mussed hair even more noticeable, and laid it over the windowsill. "Lie down over this. I'll lower you down."

The desk started to slide away from the door and she could hear Peter and Jekell grunting as they braced their weight and pushed. Renee climbed through the window, wriggled around, and hung from the sill. Eric grabbed her wrists and lowered her as far as he could reach, then let go.

She dropped about eight feet to the roof of the shack and rolled away, giving Eric room. He hit the roof about three seconds later.

"Have I mentioned how much I fucking hate heights?" he asked through gritted teeth, helping her to her feet.

"No. Really? You hate heights? But today you've been—"

"Following you through every damned window in the world, God help me." He looked up at the window they'd just climbed from, and shuddered. "At least it wasn't as far as it was when we jumped to the skyway this afternoon."

"Yeah, yeah. Come on, let's get down. I doubt those two will follow, but . . ."

"Come back here, you bitch!"

"Boy, would I like to shove the barrel of my gun in that guy's mouth," Eric muttered.

"Where *is* your gun?"

"I don't have a carry permit for this state," he admitted sheepishly.

She laughed; she couldn't help it. "Not very heroic."

"What, obeying gun laws? *Au contraire.*"

It was a perfectly still night, not a breath of wind, and thus she could hear very plainly when Jekell uttered the words that froze her blood: "Shoot them, you idiot."

"Get to the ground," Eric murmured. "Quickly." He stood protectively in front of her while she hurried to the edge of the roof.

Random's voice was uncharacteristically nervous. "I'm not shooting a woman, no matter how big a pain in my ass she's been."

"Give me that!" Jekell sounded far more focused.

She got down, rolled over, and slid over on her stomach. Again, Eric gripped her wrists. "You know him better than I do," he said, lowering her down. "Will he shoot?"

They both heard the whine of bullets at the same time. She saw Eric's shirt collar twitch and screamed at the near miss.

"Guess that answers that," he said lightly.

She took a deep, gulping breath. So close! Three inches to the right and his blood would be raining down into her face. "For sixty billion dollars, he'd shoot his grandma. Now let go and *get down here!*"

They heard a tussle, and Random shouting. Then another shot.

"Shit! Felt the wind of that one, too. Off you go." He let

go, and for the twentieth time in six hours, she dropped. Her luck finally caught up with her; she felt the stab of pain race up her ankle and settle in her knee.

"Hurry up!" she cried, trying to stand and failing. "Get down here!"

Jekell appeared interested in emptying the clip into either one of them; luckily, like most desk jockeys, he was a terrible shot. Still, she was terrified and wouldn't relax until Eric was beside her on the ground. Funny. She thought she'd been scared before today, but that was nothing to how she felt now, while the man she loved was dodging bullets.

The tree behind her was shaking, but that was the only evidence that the Jackal was killing anything. She imagined the near misses were dumb luck—hers and his.

Eric landed beside her with an "Oof!" and grabbed her hand. She yelped when he tried to pull her to her feet. "What's wrong? Are you hit?"

"My ankle. Landed wrong—can you believe it? Get—hey!" He bent and scooped her into his arms like a child. "Eric, for crying out loud, I weigh a ton. You can't haul me around like a toddler."

"Watch me."

He took two steps, and then the spot beam was in their eyes and he nearly dropped her.

"Police! Hold it right there!"

Chapter Twelve

"Ummmmm."

"Good?"

"Ohhhh, yeah. Do that again."

"Beg me."

"Please, please do that again. I'll die if you don't."

Eric leaned forward and dropped another Godiva truffle into her open mouth. Renee chewed, her eyes rolling blissfully. Chocolate was better than codeine, any day. Besides, her ankle hardly hurt anymore. A mild sprain, at worst.

He smiled at her. "Chocoholic, huh?"

"Let's put it this way: I need it like diabetics need insulin."

"I'll keep it in mind." He rolled over on his back and stretched. It was the next evening. Renee had had about fourteen hours of sleep; they were comfortably ensconced in the Hyatt and had just gorged themselves downstairs at the Oceanaire Seafood Room. She was quite sure she would never be able to look at a crab leg again.

After the police had taken their statements and let them go, Eric had insisted she accompany him to a new hotel. He checked all the exits and made her swear up and down she wouldn't slip out on him in the middle of the night. It was touching, as only rampant paranoia can be.

He yawned and pulled her close for a quick snuggle. "I still can't believe Dr. Foster called the cops," he said to the top of her head.

She swallowed the truffle and looked longingly at the gold box beside Eric. No, eight was probably enough. "Me neither. Here I thought she left us on our own, when she was actually sending for the cavalry. Thank God. I thought Dr. Jekell was going to have an embolism on the spot."

"He's lucky I didn't kick his ass on the spot," Eric said darkly. "Piece of shit crook, shooting at my girl."

"Actually, it looked to me like he was shooting at you. Badly, of course, but still . . ."

Eric got up and checked the locks one last time. Renee filched one last truffle, then reluctantly closed the box and put it on the bedside table. "You're not still worried, are you? I mean . . . it's over. Right?"

"Right. Old habits. And I don't like the way Peter Random disappeared and left Jekell holding the bag. I'd prefer not to let you out of my sight until he turns up again."

Actually, Renee quite liked the way Peter had done a quick fade when things started to go bad. Thus, there was no one to corroborate Dr. Jekell's version of events: namely, that Renee had stolen company property and tried to kill him. Since he was waving an empty gun at her as he said this, the police were skeptical, to say the least.

And when Eric showed them his credentials, and they made a few phone calls to verify his bona fides, things looked considerably worse for Dr. Jekell, who was by then shrieking like a madman.

Although she was the thief, Dr. Jekell had been arrested. The charges were attempted kidnapping, reckless endangerment, attempted murder, possession of an unlicensed handgun, and eventually assaulting a police officer. Every time Renee thought about the look on Jekell's face when the cops read him his rights, she felt like breaking into song.

"I asked you last night, before we went to sleep, but you dodged the question—where is PaceIC?"

"Right now? Your shaving kit."

"Oh. That's good. I thought—what?"

She mimed shaving her chin. "What, I have to get out hand puppets? I put. It in. Your shaving. Kit."

"The vial worth billions is next to my Remington?"

"Calm down. I'm giving it to Jennifer Hildebrandt tomorrow morning."

"Where was it before? When we were running all over the place?"

"Your shaving kit."

Eric, who had been pacing, now stopped and put his head in his hands. "You're killing me. The whole time?"

"I figured you'd never guess that when I left your room in a rage, I left PaceIC behind. Figured you wouldn't even bother to look. I'm trying to erase all tones of smugness from my voice as I say this: I was right. And with Random MIA, Jekell in jail, and Dr. Foster firmly on our side, it'll be safe there for one more night."

He laughed, shaking his head. "You're one woman in a million."

"I'm a woman in sixty billion. I liked Foster's idea. Give it to someone who can reverse engineer it, which will force Anodyne to put it on the market ASAP. Everybody wins. Except that SOB, Dr. Jekell. When he gets out of jail, let's go break his kneecaps."

"It's a date."

"I suppose I should head home tomorrow morning," Renee continued as he shut out the lights and climbed into bed. Funny how it seemed perfectly natural to share a bed with this man. If he hadn't been there, the bed would have seemed much too big. "Haven't been to my apartment all week. My cat would be dead, if I had one."

"Come with me," he coaxed. His hand slipped into her robe and cupped her left breast. "We can fly out to DC tomorrow."

"Now, why would I do that?" she teased. "We've agreed it's over."

"Wrong, m'dear. It's just beginning."

She groaned. "I can't take another week like this last one."

His thumb was rubbing over her nipple, coaxing it into stiffness. "Oh, come on," he said, and she knew he was smiling at her in the dark. "It wasn't all bad."

"There might have been one or two less sucky spots."

"How's your ankle?"

"Not too sore for what you're thinking. So that's it, huh? Good-bye, Minneapolis, hello, DC?"

"Just for a while. I want to show you the sights, introduce you to my family."

"You have family out there?"

Now his hands were sliding lower, and she wriggled closer to him and let her own hands do some wandering. "Yes. See, there's so much we don't know about each other. And I think we should spend the rest of our lives finding everything out."

"Well . . . I know you're pretty good in bed. Not that we've actually done it in a bed. And I know you don't like heights, but you don't hesitate to jump out windows for me. And I know you—ah. Yes. That's—um. Don't stop doing that."

"I won't if you won't. Say it, Renee."

"I love your dick."

A sigh in the dark. "Renee . . ."

"Oh, and the rest of you, I s'pose. But not because you've got great hands. And not because you're ridiculously good looking."

"Oh? Then why?"

She kissed him softly, sweetly, breathed in his scent, and was completely happy for the first time in a very long time. "I think, Eric, it's because you caught me," she whispered. "Now, what do you think about that?"

He showed her.

LOVELY LIES

Prologue

ICU/Oncology
Abbott Northwestern Hospital
One year earlier

"Lori . . ."

She closed her anatomy book at once and went to her mother's side. She spent so much time in this room. The smell of death, bleach, and medicine never quite left her clothes and hair. "Mom, you should be resting."

"I've been in and out of a coma for the past three weeks," her mother said with a trace of the old snap. "I can't get much more rested. Now you listen, Lori-bird. For a change, everything seems awfully clear. Like after I quit drinking wine at night! That won't last long. I don't have much time—"

"Don't talk like that," she said stonily, willing the tears not to fall. "Remission is right around the corner."

"Oh, dear. You're not doing well in medical school, are you?"

Lori laughed, the sound shocking and out of place on the ward. Well, her mother could always do that. "You know perfectly well that these things aren't always—"

"Hush up and listen," she snapped softly, tugging Lori closer. "Leave now. Tonight. It'll be over tonight. And you have to get away, Lori. Get away from both of them."

"Both . . ."

"I *know*, Lori. I've known for a long time. You should have told me—but we don't have time for that right now. I've bought you some time, all I could. You leave now."

Shocked, she took her mother's hand, which had all the weight and warmth of a dead sparrow. "I don't know what you're talking about. Will you stop? It's not funny. I'm not leaving you."

"No more time . . . for jokes. My friends—my *doctor* friends—have promised. It's over tonight. They'll see to it. Do you understand?"

She said nothing.

"Good. Then go. Get gone and stay gone. For me, Lori. More, for yourself."

"I can't—" She swallowed the rest of her sentence. Stupid— and monstrously selfish—to burden her mother with her problems now. Problems neither of them could help. "I can't go."

"You'd better. They'll be after you before the ink of my death certificate is dry. Promise."

"Mom—"

The frail grip on Lori's hand tightened. "Promise."

"I promise."

"Good. That's good." Her mother relaxed. "And don't worry, Lori. You'll find help. A random stranger, if nothing else."

"What, Mom?"

But her mother had already fallen asleep.

Obedient in all things, Lori gathered up her things and walked out of the room.

She never saw her mother again, not even in dreams.

Chapter One

Peter Random knocked back his Rusty Nail with two gulps, his gaze never leaving the filthy television screen by the bar. He clutched his lottery ticket with one hand, and raised his empty glass with the other.

"Sure you wouldn't rather have a ginger ale?" the bartender asked.

"Sure you wouldn't rather have a black eye?"

"Oooh, meee-yow! Down, kitty." Mark deftly swept away the empty glass and, in a few efficient motions, placed a fresh drink in front of Peter. "I thought you were an alcoholic."

"Alcoholics go to meetings," he said absently. *Come on, come on. Get to the winning numbers. Who cares about more corporate layoffs? Call that news? Welcome to the club, losers.* "Me, I just like the sauce."

"You're a dinosaur, Random." Mark softened the criticism with a grin. "Nobody says sauce anymore."

Peter grunted in response, but couldn't help thinking Mark had a point. He really *was* a throwback. He should have been born in the forties, been one of those hard-hearted gumshoes of the old silver screen, a gun in one hand and a shot of whiskey in the other. Some gorgeous, dangerous dame on his arm, and bad guys just behind the last corner.

Yeah.

Instead, he did background checks for a biotech firm. Checking up on overgrown geeks for a living, a thrill a minute. Correct that: He *used to* do background checks for a biotech firm. Not anymore, boys and girls. When that goody-goody snot, Renee Jardin, got PaceIC out of Anodyne and Axelrod helped her get away, Peter did a quick fade. No use hanging around—everything was about to go to shit.

He hadn't been wrong, either. Anodyne was about to go belly up, and the feds had come for the Jackal. Heh. That was almost worth losing his job. He hadn't minded trying to put the squeeze on Renee—she *did* steal Anodyne property—but toward the end, the Jackal had completely lost it. And Peter wasn't shooting nobody over some dumb medical thing, *nobody*, especially not a woman.

Seeing Jackal handcuffed, foaming like a mad dog, raving that they hadn't seen the last of him . . . yeah, that made everything worthwhile. Almost.

He didn't mind Dr. Jekell taking the fall. The asshole had put everything in motion; he *should* accept the consequences. But Peter *did* mind missing his rent payment for the second month in a row. His landlady, Mrs. O'Halloran, looked like an old-time TV grandma, all apple cheeks and spectacles and kindly, twinkling blue eyes. But she had the temper of a starving wolverine and, truth be told, he was scared to death of her. So no going back home until he had a new job.

"Hey, Mark. You guys hiring?"

The bartender laughed. "First of all, putting you in charge of the booze would be like putting a dog in charge of the Alpo. Second, we don't need a bouncer. Here come your numbers."

Peter took another gulp, then set his glass down and focused on the television. The broad pulling the balls out of the spinner looked disturbingly like Renee Jardin. Same stature and coloring, same dippy grin. Christ. That was nothing to be thinking about. Time to think about his future, the houses he'd buy with the two-point-eight million dollars in this week's Powerball. Time to think about what to name his company, his baby, his dream.

"Six," the Renee clone said sweetly to the camera. Peter didn't have to look at his ticket. He played the same numbers every week. Six, twenty, six, thirty-nine. Mama Chuck's birthday. "Twenty. Six." His fingers tightened on the ticket. *Come to papa, sweetheart!* "Forty. Ten. Those numbers again—"

"Son of a bitch," he sighed, and drained his drink.

"Maybe next week," Mark said.

"Maybe pigs will fly out of my ass."

"I have no idea," Mark said cheerfully, "but a man like you probably has several disagreeable habits."

That made him crack a smile. Wiseass punk bartender. "I don't have to take this. My left sock is older than you are."

"Most likely."

Peter pushed the rest of his drink away. "How's school?"

"Hard. You wouldn't believe how much stuff there is to memorize. I mean, I knew it'd be hard, don't get me wrong, but I had no idea." Mark whipped a rag from his belt and wiped up the condensation left on the bar. "Working here most nights doesn't help."

"Quit."

"Oh, very encouraging! You should have been a guidance counselor."

Peter shrugged. "The world has enough goddamned lawyers."

"Not the kind I'm going to be," Mark said firmly. He made Peter's dirty glass disappear and a tall glass with ginger ale and a cherry take its place. "You're thinking of high-priced defense lawyers. I'm going to get my degree, then put up a shingle back home and help people who can't afford good representation."

Peter stared at Mark, who was practically vibrating with earnest intensity, and wondered if he'd ever felt like that about anything. The kid made him tired.

He poked a finger at the ginger ale. "I don't want that. My back teeth are floating as it is."

"Very well put. Gosh, how come some lucky lady hasn't snatched you up?"

He ignored that. "How much?"

"Um . . . I'll take a twenty."

"Grasping bastard. These drinks are worth half that. And I'm not touching the pop."

"Ah, but you're tipping for exceptional service."

"My ass," he said, and left forty. Somehow, he felt the kid had earned it.

There was a woman sleeping in his backseat.

Peter looked around the dark parking lot. Yep, he was standing beside his puke-brown Ford Escort, all right. He could have sworn he'd locked it before heading to the bar, but shit, Eagan wasn't New York City. It was a mild-mannered suburb of Minneapolis, with more blond yuppies per square mile than anywhere else in the world.

He opened the back door and waited. She didn't stir. He poked her foot, which was clad in a dark blue sneaker. Her legs were bare, and she was wearing khaki shorts. In October! She had on a tattered black leather bomber jacket, but he couldn't see her face because it was buried in her arms. Her hair, from what he *could* see, was exactly poised between red and blond. He couldn't help staring. He'd always heard the phrase strawberry blond, but had never seen such a perfect example.

She wasn't a pro, taking a rest between hustles. Not unless prostitutes were wearing shorts and bulky jackets to troll for cock these days. So what the hell was she doing here?

He cleared his throat and looked around the parking lot again. He was half hoping some geek would bounce up to the car and say, "Oh, right! Forgot my girlfriend. Here, let me take her off your hands. Sorry for the inconvenience."

Nope. Not a soul, and she didn't move.

He leaned in to tap her in the middle of the back, and then he got a whiff. Strawberries and rum. She wasn't asleep, she was passed out.

Drunk.

In his car.

"Well, shit," he said aloud. What the hell was he supposed

to do? Call the cops? Dump her out and leave her in the parking lot? Take her home?

The cops were out—too many of them had questions about the attempted murder thing with Renee. He could pull the broad out and leave her, but . . .

The woman in his car began to snore.

"Fuck it," he said, and slammed the car door, being careful not to catch any of her curls.

Chapter Two

Peter staggered up the front steps with the drunk bim in his arms—she was dead weight, completely zonked. He glanced over his shoulder to the house directly across the street from his. Thank you, Jesus! All the lights were out. His landlady was asleep, no doubt storing up her evil powers to use on him in daylight. There were some real benefits to coming home from a bar at one-thirty in the morning.

Peter stared at his locked front door and finally draped what's-her-face over the porch railing, belly down, while he fished for his keys. He got the door unlocked in another moment, then grabbed her under the armpits and dragged her inside. Cripes, if any of his neighbors saw him, they'd be on the phone to the cops before you could say serial killer. And more attention from the boys in blue he did *not* need.

"This is nuts," he muttered under his breath. Booger, his cat, yowled in agreement from her perch on the living room sofa. "Hang in there, baby. I'll feed you in a second." He hoisted the stray du jour into his arms and carried her to his bedroom. Great. On top of everything else, he was sleeping on the fucking couch tonight.

He dumped her unceremoniously on the bed, half hoping she would wake up, but she simply flopped back over on her stomach and went on snoring. Not cute little ladylike snores, either. Real buzz saws.

Nothing to do now but wait. And feed the damned cat, of course.

Lori Jamieson rolled over and stared at a ceiling that was completely unfamiliar. Where in the world?

She blinked, puzzled, then sat up, massaged her pounding temples, and nearly screamed when she saw the man straddling the chair at the foot of the bed. As it was, a muffled squeak escaped her lips, and she felt her heart rate double. Her headache, which had been mildly painful, suddenly became a skull buster.

"Well, finally," the man said. He was alarming looking, to say the least. Big, quite big, with the palest blue eyes she'd ever seen, and the thickest black hair. He was dressed in faded blue jeans and a white open-throated shirt. She could see the fine black hair on his knuckles, and the lines bracketing his eyes. On most people, those would be called laugh lines. Not on this one . . . he looked really mean.

Good.

"Look who's awake," he said, drumming his fingers on his knee.

"I—you scared me."

"Uh-huh. What's doing, sweetheart? Why were you in my car?"

"Fine, thanks, and you?"

"Oh, you're gonna lecture me on manners? You get drunk and pass out in my backseat, but I'm the troglodyte?"

"Yes." And, for the first time since the news of her mother's probate, she giggled, which caused him to raise an eyebrow at her. "Sorry, not too polite, right? It's just that it's been kind of a long—aagghh!"

The ugliest cat she had ever seen strolled into the bedroom. She tried not to stare, but she couldn't help it. It looked like a cat that had been run over, then put back together by an evil genius. Its eyes were two different colors, one a baleful green, the other a crystal blue. Its fur was a mottled brown, and its feet were white, except for the back left leg, which was reddish-orange. It was missing an ear, and half its tail.

"What happened to your cat? Or giant rat? Or whatever?"

"It's not mine," he said quickly. Too quickly, she decided. "I don't even know what it's doing here. I hate cats. Shoo! Get lost!"

The cat gave him a long stare, then slowly walked out.

"Just a stray, huh?"

"It sneaks in when I'm not here. I have to find the crawl hole it keeps using and close it up."

"Maybe you should take it to the pound."

He nearly gasped. "They gas cats there every week! Uh— also, I'm too damned busy. Yeah, I—enough about the cat. Let's hear your story. Why were you in my car?"

"I got it mixed up with mine," she said. The cat chat had given her time to think up something. "I have an Escort, too. I knew I was too drunk to get home by myself, so I thought I'd sleep for a while, then drive home."

"Bullshit," he said. "Mine was the only Escort in the parking lot. So unless you got the bar mixed up with the Laundromat, you're lying. Let's try something simple, like your name."

"Debbie."

"Strike two, Red." He held up something black. Shocked, she realized it was her billfold. "Your name is Lori Jamieson, and everybody is looking for you. Did you know the cops think you've been kidnapped?"

Her mouth popped open. "You went through my things while I was asleep?"

"Sure."

"You bastard!"

"Sure. It's good that you know something about me. And I know a few things about you. I know your name's Lori, I know you're a student at the U, I know you're in deep shit, and I know you're a liar."

"I—you—" Had she ever been so angry and so frightened at the same time? She didn't think so. She didn't know whether to throw something at him or hide under the bed.

"So. One more time. And, Lori, sugarpie, do *not* make me ask you a fourth time." He grinned. He had a lot of teeth. She suppressed a shiver. "Who the hell are you, and why did you pick me?"

"Oh, no."

"Come on, don't play coy now. Out with it. Don't make me throw you and the cat in the same sack."

She tried to think, but it was so hard . . . her head was pounding in time with her heartbeat, and the room started to spin like a merry-go-round gaining speed. She raised a trembling hand to her mouth. "Wh-where's the bathroom?"

His forehead creased as he frowned at her. "I'd assume this was another sorry-ass stall tactic, but you don't look too good."

"I don't feel—hurp! Too good. I'm *not* stalling, you shouldn't . . . ohhhhhh . . ."

She was amazed at how quickly he moved for such a big man. In a flash, he'd pulled her off the bed, yanked her across the room, and tossed her into a bathroom.

"You make a mess," he said, turning on the light and then closing the door, "you're cleaning it up. I have no idea where the mop is."

She staggered toward the toilet. "Don't worry about m—urgh!"

The final humiliation in a long week of them, she thought, and threw up so hard she saw white spots in front of her eyes.

Chapter Three

Peter could still hear Lori shoutin' at the floor—what had she eaten, an antelope?—and decided not to knock just yet. Instead, he crept into the kitchen and gave Booger half of the fresh tuna steak he'd picked up from the fish market yesterday. It was ridiculously expensive, and the place was only about sixty miles out of his way, but the cat seemed to like it.

Between overtipping bartenders and feeding Booger high on the hog, it was no wonder most of his money had run out. *Peter, old pal,* he thought ruefully, *you're a classic sucker.*

"Hurry up before she comes out. Eat faster, damn it. God, did you see her face? Did you see her *eyes?*"

What he hadn't noticed while she was facedown on his bed was how extraordinarily pretty she was. He already knew she had nice legs. Real legs, too, great old-fashioned gams like you saw on Marilyn and Rita, not the stringy, thin legs women worked to get these days. And her body was pretty good—she was a little too thin, but nothing that couldn't be fixed with a few milkshakes and steak dinners. Decent rack. But her face . . . wow.

She had the cutest little nose, sprayed almost artistically with a fine network of freckles. He couldn't help it; he had counted them while they were talking. Well, while he was talking . . . she hadn't said much. She had the lushest lips he'd seen since he quit subscribing to *Penthouse*. Her mouth was red and pouty, even without makeup, and begged for kisses. And her eyes . . . her eyes were the color of the fog coming in off the ocean. He'd never seen gray eyes before.

When she sat up and opened those amazing eyes, he'd nearly fallen off the chair. He hadn't felt such a stroke of such urgent lust in—when *had* he let that subscription lapse?

He expected a tiresome litany . . . who are you, where am I, can you drive me home, sorry for your trouble, blah-blah. Instead, the line of bullshit she'd trotted out was interesting, to say the least. She was up to something, all right. The real question was, did she just pick a car at random, or did she pick *him*?

As soon as that antelope was all the way out, he'd find out.

Booger finished her tuna and twined around his legs, so he picked her up and carried her to her room. "Stay in here," he said into her one ear. "Take a nap." She purred against his chest, then jumped from his arms to her twin bed, curled up, and closed one eye. It always cracked him up when she slept with her green eye open. Other people would probably find it disturbing, he supposed.

He went back out, through the kitchen and down the hall, and into his bedroom. He knocked on the bathroom door. "Red? You gonna live?"

"Unfortunately," he heard her groan.

He grinned in spite of himself.

"D'you have any aspirin?"

"Yeah. How many you want?"

"Six hundred."

"How about a glass of 7-Up instead?"

"I'll accept that. On a trial basis, anyway. I'm really, really sorry, but I'm going to use your toothbrush now."

"Thanks for the warning."

When she tottered into the kitchen, he silently held a chair back for her and she sank into it with a grateful sigh.

"Peter, this is wonderful," she said with what he assumed

was sincere gratitude. He'd taken a minute to fix toast and pour her a glass of pop. "Thanks."

"No problem." He sat across from her, waited until she took a bite, then added pleasantly, "I never told you my name."

After he'd given her a modified Heimleich and the toast chunk had gone flying from her esophagus into the living room, he made her sit down and drink her pop while he grabbed the errant chunk with a napkin and chucked it into the garbage.

"Don't do that ever again," she said sternly.

"Well, shit, I did think you were gonna choke."

"And you did so tell me your name."

"Nope."

"Well, shit."

"Yup."

She put her glass down and rested her face on the Flint-stones placemat. "I screwed this up all the way around," she muttered.

"There were about twenty ways you coulda done it better," he agreed.

Her head snapped up and she glared at him. Then she clutched her head. "Ouch! And thanks a lot."

"So are you gonna tell me what you're doing here, or what?"

She bit her lower lip, which made it swell, almost as if she was asking for a kiss. He stared and tried to stop his mouth from hanging open. Did this broad have any idea how fine looking she was?

"Can I take a shower first?" she stalled.

"Oh, for—you don't have anything to change into."

"I can borrow one of your T-shirts."

"Is that so?"

She smiled at him. Great smile—made her whole face light up. It was like watching the sun come over a hill. He fought the urge to promise her anything. "I've got you now, Peter. You're too curious to throw me out."

"Well, that's a fact," he admitted. "I guess I'll rustle up some clothes for you, then."

"And more to drink?" she asked hopefully.

He scowled. "OK." *Peter, you are such a sucker.*

Forty minutes later—what did she do in there, wash every millimeter six times?—she was at the table again, her long hair wrapped in a towel, wearing his Come Along Quietly T-shirt and a pair of sweatpants cut out at the knees. They were so long on her the holes were closer to her ankles.

"That's much better," she said, polishing off her third glass. "You know, the reason hangovers are so painful is dehydration."

"Tell me about it. Now, out with it."

"That's it? Out with it?"

"Lady, you have *no* idea how patient I've been. Trust me, it's totally out of character. Now spill it."

"OK." She took a deep breath and looked him square in the eyes. "I want to hire you for protection."

"Bodyguard work? Pass."

"But you need the job!"

"Do I?" He was starting to get nervous and tried to control it. When he got nervous, he hit and kicked and stuff broke. People, too, sometimes. And he didn't want to scare Red. But the fact was, she had staked him out. She knew his name and knew he was out of work. And she was as twitchy as an epileptic who'd skipped medication. It was nerve-racking. "You seem to know about me, but I don't know much about you, Red."

"Lori."

"Right. Except that you've gone missing and your family called the—"

"They're not my family!" The empty glass went sailing past his left ear and shattered against the fridge. As he watched, her pupils shrank to almost nothing. Adrenaline rush. Fight or flight. Now *that* was interesting. "Don't you call them that," she hissed. "Neither one of them is related to me. They only

called the police to track me down. My only family died a year ago."

"OK. Take it easy. That glass was super expensive."

It worked; she smiled a little. "It was an old jelly jar. Unless you buy all your glasses at the Smuckers factory."

He turned around and looked at the mess on the floor. "You got a good arm, Red, give you that. But if you think I'm sweeping that shit up, you're nuts."

"I'll take care of it. I'm sorry—I've got a terrible temper. My mom's temper." The smile dropped away as if it had never been there. "She's dead."

"OK."

"And I'm in trouble."

"I figured."

"And I want you to watch out for me and help me."

"Red—"

"Lori."

"—I don't do bodyguard stuff. Not to say I couldn't use the job, because I could, I mean, as long as we're being square with each other, right? But I don't want a job where getting shot or knifed is part of the job description. You want me to check someone out, I'm your fella. You want me to mangle people giving you trouble, just point 'em out and I'll put foot to ass. But dogging your footsteps and jumping in front of you to take a bullet in my teeth . . . nope."

"You won't have to take a bullet. I just need you to keep them off me while I figure out what to do," she said. Her expression was earnest and hopeless at the same time. "I thought they were out of my life, but now that the will's finally been read they're back, worse than ever. I'm not surprised . . . but it makes me tired."

"Who's 'they'?"

"My mother's second husband and his son."

Not, he noticed, *my stepfather and stepbrother.* "Why are they so interested in you all of a sudden?"

"They want the money."

"The—unbelievable!" He got up and walked around the

kitchen, careful to avoid the broken glass. "What is it with you broads and having to steal stuff? That's all I need, another sticky-fingered bim in my life."

"I didn't steal anything!" she said hotly. Her palm slapped the table with a sharp crack. He ducked, but she didn't toss the plate. "It's my mother's money. She left it to me. And those two bastards want a chunk. They'll take it all, if they can."

"Well, if your mama's will said it's yours, then they can't touch it."

"They can if something happens to me."

"Oh, here we go again. Back to bullet catching."

"I just need you to watch my back while I get rid of the money."

He was having a little trouble following her. "Get *rid* of it?"

"Yes. If I give it away, Ed and Conrad will lose interest in me. They won't be happy, of course, but they'll leave me alone. And that's all I want. It's all I ever wanted."

"That's nice, but you're not making a lot of sense. You want to ditch your inheritance? All of it? That's crazy. It's yours. We—I mean, *you* can figure out how to get those guys off your trail. Don't be too hasty, for Christ's sake."

She shook her head so hard the towel came undone, spilling wet red-gold strands to her shoulders. "My mother's money came from *her* father. All his life, he held it over her head like a whip. Do this, go there, do that, and if you don't, no money. It made her miserable. And now it's making me miserable. I don't want it. I'm getting rid of it."

"Well, maybe I could help you out with that. How much moolah are we talking about here?"

"Nine hundred thousand dollars. Give or take a few thousand."

He sat down before his knees unhinged.

Chapter Four

Lori resisted the impulse to roll her eyes. As soon as she'd told him the amount, she could see the dollar signs pop up in his pupils.

"Well, shoot, Red, it's your lucky day!"

She sighed. "Don't, Peter."

He tilted the chair back, stretched, and then brought it down on all four legs with a crash. "I'll be glad to take that nasty inheritance off your hands," he said, actually rubbing his hands together with glee. "Yeah, your dead mama was a real jerk to put such a burden on you. Luckily, Uncle Peter is here!"

She tried not to shudder. "Did you know when you try to sound warm and caring, you're actually twice as terrifying?"

"Well." He appeared to mull that one over. "I don't get a lot of practice."

"That's why I picked you. And I'm sorry, but you can't have it. I mean, I'll keep some of it back for your fee. But I have to give it away in chunks. Do you know why my mother was disowned for so long?"

"No," he said, bored.

"She wanted to be a doctor. And so she was. And when she had her MD, she spent the rest of her life helping as many people as she could. This horrified my grandfather, who was sure she would catch some poverty disease from the masses and bring it home to the mansion. If I just—splat!—plopped her money down in one spot, it'd almost be dishonoring her memory."

"Bullshit. Give it to—I can't believe I'm saying this—the Red Cross or something. They'll spread it around for you."

Lori shook her head. "My mother would want me to go out and see a situation for myself, then write a check for the appropriate amount. All over the city, or the state, or the world."

"Why didn't your mom give it away?"

"She couldn't. If she wouldn't spend it the way Grandpa dictated, she had to put it in a trust for me. But his control over it only extended so far, and now I'm free to do with it what I like."

He thought that one over. "So she did that, OK, but . . . you think your mom knew you'd give her dough away?"

"I'm sure of it."

"Well, you're both nuts. But you're the boss."

She smiled. All at once, her headache vanished. Pop! The soda finally kicking in, or sheer relief? "Decided to work for me, have you?"

"Sure. And help you with the biggest shopping spree in the damn world. But don't forget to save a chunk for me."

"Ah, now we'll get down to it. How much?"

"Um . . ." He tapped his chin. His fingers were as large as sausages. Really, he was a terrifying creature to behold. And thank goodness. "To be at your side, to keep you safe from the booger your mom married—"

She laughed at that; she couldn't help it. If ever there was a walking booger in the world, it was Ed.

"—that's gonna take up a lot of my time. Sooooo . . . a hundred grand."

She snorted. "I can't imagine this will take more than a few days of your time."

"OK," he said with an air of generosity that was utterly bogus, "Fifty grand."

"I'll give you two thousand for each day. But that covers your expenses, too."

"Done," he said quickly. He spit in his hand and then held it out to her. "Shake on it."

She shrank back from his glistening palm. "I'm not touching your hand until you boil it."

He shrugged and wiped his palm on his pants. "Suit yourself." He grinned, and she had a sudden glimpse of the sharp mind lurking beneath the Neanderthal exterior.

He did that just to see how I'd react, she thought. *What a very strange man.*

"So, what next?"

"I need to pick up the checkbook from my lawyer's. He's supposed to get it first thing tomorrow morning. In the meantime, I have to stay out of sight."

"You have a checkbook for this money?"

"It's in a trust. The trust has been moved, per my mother's will, to an account, and I'm supposed to take possession of the checkbook for it tomorrow. Do you know what the name of the trust is?"

He'd been interested while they were talking numbers, but now he was bored again. "Now, how the hell would I know that?" He got up, went to the door opposite the table, opened it, and pulled out a broom. He walked over to her and, as she stood, handed it to her. "Clean while you talk, sweetie."

"It's called Random Acts."

"OK."

"Don't you think that's amazing? Your last name is Random!"

He looked at her expressionlessly. "Oh, so I was fated to help you?"

She started to sweep and tried to hold onto her temper. One tantrum was plenty. "My mom died, and I go into hiding for a year. About the time I need to get moving, you lose your job. I'm desperate. I see your picture in the paper—the story about that bio company that lost their invention, or whatever. And your picture was sort of glaring up at me. You looked bad, and you looked mean. And your last name was Random. Random! I mean, come on! I *had* to track you down. It was like fate was hitting me over the head with that newspaper."

"So fate's some sort of celestial dog trainer? Ha! I don't believe in anything but coincidences. So you should get the stars out of your eyes, Red. And sweep, don't flip. You're tossing broken glass all over the place."

She gritted her teeth and swept. *Well, what did you expect? You wanted a hard man. And that's exactly what you got. So don't cry about it now.*

Good advice. She hoped she'd be able to take it.

"Good God!" She stopped short and Peter ran into her. The shock of his body nearly caused her to yell again. She'd never heard him coming up behind her. Quiet as a cat, and solid as a rock. Too bad he had no soul. "Are these all yours?"

"No, I run a video store out of my living room. 'Course they're all mine." He edged around her and spread his arms like a badass game show host. "Cool, huh?"

The entire east wall of the living room was solid movies. About two-thirds were standard VHS, and the other third was all DVDs. She guessed she was looking at roughly six thousand movies.

"You want to watch something?"

"Er . . . not especially."

His face fell. She was so surprised, she blurted without thinking, "I wouldn't mind going out to a movie, though."

"Really? Mall of America?"

She tried not to wince. But this was the first thing he'd shown any animation about, besides the money. And he *was* helping her out. Even though she was paying him, she was still grateful.

"Red? Do you?"

"Sure. I've been on the run for the last few days. I'd love to—uh—" *Expose myself to the masses at the largest shopping mall on the planet.* "I'd love to."

"Great! And don't worry," he added, correctly reading her expression. "No one's gonna be looking for you there, of all places. And if anyone is, I can handle them."

"I'm sure there won't be any problems," she said doubtfully.

Chapter Five

If anyone had told me Peter Random loved window shopping, I'd have said they needed to change their medication.

"Red! Hey! Over here! Look at that, a whole store full of bikinis. And it's practically wintertime!"

"Truly amazing," she agreed dutifully. "Peter . . . how long have you lived in Minnesota?"

"I was born in South Minneapolis and never got around to leaving," he replied, now chomping cheese samples from Cheez It, Da Kops.

"Oh." So much for her tourist theory. In her experience, the natives didn't get terribly excited about the Mall anymore. Never the mall, always the Mall, so you could hear the capital letter.

Oh, sure, there had been lots of speculation and traffic when it was built over a decade ago, but locals got used to anything in ten years. Even the biggest mall in the universe. She herself hadn't been here in four years.

He grabbed her hand and pulled her down toward the escalator. "Come on, let's shake a leg."

"Peter, the movie doesn't start for half an hour."

"Yeah, but . . ." She was a step above him on the escalator, and he looked up at her earnestly. "We can't miss any of the previews."

"Heaven forbid."

Lori didn't know whether to be annoyed or charmed. Apparently her troubles—and they were pretty significant, thank you!—had rolled right off Peter's shoulders. He had a job, he was getting paid, end of discussion. Or interest. It was—well, she didn't know what. She wasn't attracted to him. He was a means to an end. Right? Right.

On the other hand, when was the last time she'd gone to the movies? Not this year, certainly. Possibly not even the last. As if the nightmare of her mother's death and probate hadn't been enough to keep her occupied, she was also in her fourth year of med school. She'd had to drop out, of course, but hopefully she could make up the work next quarter. Once all this was over.

Oh, if only all this was over.

Regardless, if she was forced to hang out in limbo, it was nice to be entertained. And Peter was, if nothing else, entertaining.

As it was on any Sunday, the Mall was ridiculously crowded. Throngs of people packed the walkways, the escalators, the stores. Peter didn't seem to notice or care; he was holding her wrist and shouldering his way through packs of people. She had to admit it was an efficient means of getting where you needed to go.

There was a group of older teenagers clustered around the ticket booth, and Lori instinctively tightened up.

She wasn't a racist. She wasn't. At least, she didn't think she was. She would have been nervous if the four—no, five—youths slouched in torn clothes and bristling with jewelry and funny haircuts had been Caucasian. Even the smallest probably outweighed her by twenty pounds. It was just one of those things a lone woman accepted—you took care when you were around a group of boys-not-quite-men.

As she and Peter got closer, it was obvious they were arguing about what movie to see. Peter waited impatiently while the dialogue floated over them.

"—sequel to the *Terminator*—"

"—fuck you, that's a chick flick—"

"—fuck *you,* it *ain't*—"

"—fuck all of you, let's get in there—"

"Yeah," Peter said. "Decide now or make room, boys."

Their arguing stopped as if Peter had hit a switch. Lori felt the weight of their menace as they gave him their full attention.

"We'll move when we're done, homes," the tallest of them said in a curiously gentle voice. "Best you wait 'til we're through."

"*Homes?* Nobody says homes anymore, pal. Next you'll be telling me about your crib in the hood." Peter laughed. *Laughed!* Lori wondered if she had time to pray for a swift death.

The tall one blinked in surprise, then said, still speaking quietly, "Oh, man, you don't want to fuck with us. You jus' don't. So stand still and be quiet and we'll move when we fucking well want to."

"How about instead I shove your head so far up your ass, you'll be able to lick your own colon?" Peter asked this in a perfectly bored tone, as if he truly didn't care whether they fought or not. Probably he didn't.

"Colon?" one of the others exclaimed.

"Oh, man, you done it now. You—"

Peter, who had been stifling a yawn, suddenly straightened up and speared the tall one with a glare. "I know you. You hang out on Chuck's block. What are you doing clogging up the line and making trouble for yourself?" He tsk'ed a few times and then added with cheerful relish, "Guess I'll be telling Mama Chuck on you. *All* of you."

Thunderstruck silence, followed by a chaotic chorus Lori could barely follow.

"—do that, man—"

"—kill our asses just like—"

"—didn't mean nothing—"

"—Mama beat my head so bad—"

"I know you," the one Lori took to be the leader said. A smile bloomed on his face, throwing his cheekbones into relief, which transformed him from sullen thug to Egyptian prince. "You're the Random Man!"

A new chorus:

"—shit, fucking Random Man!"

"—Mama's favorite, and she don't—"

"—that dude is the *haps*—"

"—mess with Random—"

—broken by Peter's, "Jesus, shut up! Stop talking all at once, you're giving me a headache." He jabbed the leader with a forefinger. "You. Stop pulling shit. Move when people ask you to move. Don't make me hurt you."

The boy—close to a man; Lori pegged him at about nineteen—held up his hands, palms out. She noticed they were heavily callused. He really was extraordinary, with liquid brown eyes and cheekbones she could have cut herself on. He was almost as tall as Peter, but lean as a blade. "Hey, we all do that, and you don't tell Mama, okay?"

"Yeah, fine. Get lost. Go find an old lady and help her across the street."

"The only old lady we know is Mama Chuck," one of the others piped up. He was teeny—both in stature and age—and had startling blue eyes in a dark face. A scar slashed across his cheek and buried itself in his hairline. "And if we try to help her across some street, she'll bust our heads."

Peter laughed. "You're right. And you'd deserve it, too. The day she needs help from some punk is the day I lock her in a retirement home."

Like a dark tide, the group moved back to make room for them. "You ain't *never*," the tall one said, still smiling. "Unless you want your own head busted."

"Yeah, yeah. So long, fellas."

There was a chorus of good-byes, and they reached the ticket window without further incident. Lori had about a thousand questions, but bit her tongue.

"Two for *Love At Random*. And don't start," he said, pointing at her. "It doesn't mean anything."

She folded her arms across her chest and raised her eyebrows at him. "You don't think it's weird that that's the only movie we could agree on?"

"No. I don't care what we see, and that's the one we picked. Let's not mix up the facts, Red."

"Lori," she snapped.

"Sixteen dollars," the ticket taker said from her cage.

Peter looked at her expectantly.

"What?" she said. "I don't have any money."

"Oh, for—here," he said, fishing out a twenty dollar bill and shoving it into the ticket taker's cage. "Richest bim in the Twin Cities, and she welches on the movie tickets," he added under his breath.

"Poor baby," she said, and laughed.

His frown disappeared. "You got a great laugh," he said grudgingly. "A guy could fall in love."

She was so surprised, she could say nothing in response.

"I was a little worried about those boys."

Peter paused before tossing a handful of popcorn in his mouth. "They were just kids from my old neighborhood."

"You weren't scared of them?"

"Why would I be?" he asked, honestly surprised. "Shit, why would you be? Let me tell you something about the young black man in America, Red: He's more scared of you than you are of him."

"Spoken like a man who outweighs me by seventy pounds. Of course *you* weren't scared; you can fight. And how in the world would you know what the young black man thinks about anything? You make African-Americans sound like frightened rattlers."

"Don't call us that. For all you know, those kids' folks came from Jamaica. African-American." He snorted. "PC bullshit."

She said nothing, just raised her eyebrows at him. He laughed. "Oh, hell, busted again. Well, here it is: The whole time I was growing up, I thought I was black. And old habits are the worst to break."

"Really?"

"Sure. The woman I called Mama was black, all my friends were black, and just about everyone at my school was black. So I figured I must be, too, just where no one could see. I had to get into a few fights to prove my point, but that was all right."

"What, you thought you just weren't getting as much sun as everyone else in the neighborhood?" she teased.

"No," he replied seriously, "but it wasn't anything I worried about. And after a while, most people let it go. Mama Chuck said I belonged to her, and nobody crossed my mama."

"Well, then." Lori took a sip of her Pepsi.

"That's it? That's all you got to say?"

"Pretty much." She thought for a moment. "Yes, that's it. I am empty of comments."

"Oh." He seemed pleased. "Most people try to talk me out of it. You know. When I tell them I'm black and The Man's getting me down."

She managed to lock back the giggle. "Well, they're not in your shoes, are they?"

His face lit up and he slapped his leg. "See, that's what I always say!"

"Your mother—Mama Chuck—she sounds like a good woman. I mean, she raised you, and it sounds like she's still raising kids. If you knew those teenagers."

Tired of reaching over for popcorn, he snatched the bucket out of her lap and put it on his knee. "Oh, yeah. She'll never

stop. Can't resist a stray, that's her thing. Lucky for me! I don't
know what I would have done if she hadn't of taken me in.
Shit, she took me in when my own father—"

Long pause.

"When your own father?" she prompted.

"Never mind. Um, look, the previews are starting."

That was the last he spoke for the next two hours.

Chapter Six

"Maybe that wasn't such a good idea," Peter said out of nowhere.

Lori glanced at him in surprise. They were back at his apartment, finishing the pizza he'd ordered. And paid for, she thought with an internal chuckle.

"Not a good . . . why? It was . . ." Fun? Scary? Educational? ". . . entertaining."

"And dumb. I saw all the people looking at you. You stand out, even in a crowded mall." He was staring at her moodily, which was unnerving, to say the least. "Nobody can mistake that hair color, and if they get close enough to see your eyes . . ." He shook his head. "Dumb idea. And I know better."

She dropped her pizza slice and sputtered in surprise. "They—you—they were looking at you, Peter, not me! You're so big, people can't help but look." She'd seen it; how could she have missed it? The double takes, and the rubberneckers craning to get a better look. Of course he was forbidding looking. Who wouldn't stop to stare? "I'd think you'd be used to it by now."

He peered at her closely, almost as if he were looking straight into her brain. "Jeez, and you actually believe it! Red, don't you know? You're gorgeous. You could work for *Penthouse,* make the really big bucks."

"Uh . . . thank you. I'm almost positive that was a compliment. But you're wrong. My hair's too blond to be red, and too red to be blond. My eyes are so light they're really no color at all. Bo-ring. And I'm too bony."

"You could stand to gain some weight, but that's about it. About the rest, you're wrong. Dead wrong."

"I don't think we should be talking about this," she said solemnly. "It's inappropriate."

"Also, you're cute as hell when you blush."

"I'm not blushing," she snapped. "It's a residual effect from my hangover."

He chortled and got up to toss their paper plates into the garbage. "When's this lawyer's office open?"

"Eight AM."

"OK, so we got . . ." He glanced at the clock above the stove. ". . . twelve hours to kill. Wanna play Nude Twister?'

"No."

"How about Nude Twenty Questions?"

"How about not."

"Internal conflict!" he said suddenly, startling her.

"What? Do we have to take our clothes off to play?"

"No, no. I just put my finger on what was wrong with that chick flick we saw this afternoon. I mean, after Sandra Bullock's character solved the mystery, Tom Cruise's character shoulda gone on his merry way. There was no reason for them to get together, but they did anyway. It didn't ring right."

"You—uh—you give a lot of thought to movies, don't you?"

"Greatest art form in the history of the planet."

"Even *Starship Troopers*?"

"What's wrong with *Starship Troopers*?" he said defensively. "It's got everything—war, true love, broken hearts, heroic deaths, good triumphing over bad."

"You're right. A hundred percent right. A splendid cinematic tale. Really!"

"Good," he replied with an evil grin. "Then you won't mind if we watch it. Right now."

"Ugh. I mean, yippee!"

"Red, I swear . . ." He walked into the living room, shaking his head. "You are the worst liar."

He was on her, he was hurting her, and she couldn't make him stop, would have to take it, take him, and oh, where was her mother, and why wasn't she saving her?

Con's face was above her, twisted with lust, with hate, his knee between her thighs, shoving, pushing, hurting her, and she bit her lips until they bled to lock back the begging and pleading she wanted to pour forth.

And in the background, her stepfather's voice, "What, now? You can't do that now, her mother will be home from the hospital any minute." But he wouldn't stop, wouldn't get off her, wouldn't—

"Red?"

—and now his hands were on her shoulders, shaking her, but he was uncharacteristically gentle, and she was surprised even as she was grateful, even as she was—

"Red?"

—awake.

She sat up with a gasp. The room whirled about her in the dark, adding to her disorientation. Where was she? Was her mother nearby? What had happened to her? Was she in the mansion? Was her stepfather home? Where was Con? *Where was Con?*

"Where is he?" she asked muzzily. "I have to see his eyes. If I see his eyes, I'll know."

"Nobody here but us out-of-work bums, Red."

She could barely see him in the dark. Odd, how that huge shape looming over her in the dark wasn't in the least frightening. "P—Peter?"

"Bad dream? Dumb question, 'course it was. Sounds like you had a real fun childhood." In the dark, his voice was rough and amused at the same time.

"I—I'm sorry. Did I wake you? I must have. Is the movie over? We're in your apartment, right?"

"Uh-huh. It's not your fault, though."

Her mother's exact words. She looked up at him. "What? What did you say?"

"It's not your fault. It's this fucking couch, it's evil. It gives everyone nightmares. C'mere." He bent and lifted her easily, then carried her back to the bedroom. He was shirtless, clad only in boxer shorts, and when she rested her cheek against his chest it was like resting against a warm, breathing boulder.

He set her down on the bed and awkwardly pulled the covers over her. He cleared his throat, as if about to speak, then simply stepped away.

She leaned forward and grabbed his arm. "Don't leave me alone in the dark," she whispered. She could hardly see his face in the gloom, but the sheer bulk of his body was comforting.

She heard him shift his weight. "Uh, I sorta have to."

"Please."

"Lori, I can't share a bed with you and not jump you. Sorry, but you're gorgeous and I'm a pig and that's the way it is."

"That's fine."

"Yeah, I know, I should—what'd you say?"

"I said that's fine."

His big hand closed over hers, and then he was—no!—gently prying her fingers away from his arm. "Sorry, Red. I must be out of my mind. I can't believe I'm doing this. I can't believe I'm *saying* this. But you're not yourself. Shit, I'm not myself."

"Peter . . ."

"Thanks, though," he added hastily. "I mean, I'm a lucky guy, don't get the wrong idea. It's the nicest offer I've had in— what year is this?"

"I'm in perfect control of myself," she said coolly. "And you work for me, I believe." She reached again, found the waistband of his shorts, pulled. "Last chance, Random."

She was proud of herself; she knew she sounded tough and calm. But inwardly she couldn't stop shouting, begging, *Oh please please please don't leave me alone in the dark, you'll be big and you'll be rough but I don't care, just stay and hold me after, I only want that, please, just that.*

He came to her, then, with a long sigh that might have been surrender.

She glanced at the clock. Two twenty-two in the morning. By two-thirty, they'd be snuggling, and she could have what she craved so badly.

Chapter Seven

He wasn't rough.

He was a revelation.

She had braced herself for fumbling and panting and dim pain and bad breath, for that was what she knew, and how she'd been initiated into this oddly tiresome act.

Instead, it had been like flying.

His mouth, as he took her in his arms and kissed her, was surprisingly gentle. He kissed her for an age, and when she sighed, his tongue slipped into her mouth.

Still kissing her, he caught the edge of her T-shirt and, instead of jerking it up to her neck, simply bunched the fabric in his fist and rubbed it across her nipples. She squirmed at the sensation—he was touching her breasts, but she could feel it in her stomach. Meanwhile, he kissed the delicate flesh behind her ears, then caught her earlobe in his mouth and sucked.

"Whoa!" she said, as a bolt of pure pleasure hit her between the legs. At least, that's what it felt like. She had no idea there was a nerve connecting her ear and her vulva. Today was a day for surprises, it seemed.

Peter was already backing off. "Right, right. Bad idea. Told you. I'll just be in the shower for about half an hour or so—"

She grabbed his shoulders and yanked him down to her.

"More," she said. Her eyes had adjusted to the dark and she could see his wary expression. "Do more."

His forehead smoothed out and he laughed. "You're weird."

"Less talking. More touching."

"OK, Red."

"Lori."

"Sorry, Red—ow! Don't bite. Well, OK, bite, but give a guy some warning next time."

"It's not Red," she complained as he bent down and kissed her stomach. "It's not even blond."

"Yeah, yeah."

"Well, it's not."

"Are we gonna talk about your hair, or fu—uh, have sex?"

"Can't we do both?" she asked primly, and laughed as he tickled her stomach. He eased her—well, his—sweatpants down, tossed them over the bed, and found her bare. He stroked the smooth skin of her legs, cupped her calves in his hands, then bent and nuzzled the tuft of hair between her legs.

"Red," he said, his breath warm on her thighs.

"Now cut that out."

"Well, it is. Quite a bit darker than what's on your head, in fact." His hands were between her knees, spreading them apart, and he made a greedy sound, low in his throat, as she parted before his gaze. "Gorgeous, too. Like a glistening pink pearl."

Before she could reply—not that she had any idea what to say—he had bent his head and she could feel him kissing her slick flesh. She closed her eyes, enjoying the subtly sensual feeling, but they flew open when his tongue darted out and caressed her clitoris, which instantly began to throb. There was nothing subtle about *that* sensation. It was glorious and it demanded her full attention.

His tongue was darting and licking, and when she felt it actually snake inside her she thought she would implode. As it was, she threw her head back and arched her back, digging her heels into the mattress to brace her legs. She could smell a lovely musk in the air. *We're making that smell,* she thought dazedly.

"Christ, you taste good," he muttered. "Like flowers in the ocean." She felt his thumbs spreading her apart, and then he was nuzzling her clit while licking at the same time, and she groaned. "Close?"

"Wh-what?"

"Never mind." Now he was sucking on her clit while his tongue swirled and whirled, and she felt warmth explode in her belly and radiate downward. She was arching toward him, offering as much of herself as she could, and then she felt her orgasm bloom inside her like a black orchid and cried out at the ceiling.

"I love that sound," he said, his tone pure male satisfaction. He came up beside her and pulled the T-shirt over her head. "Good?"

"Oh, God, yes."

"Not too fast?"

"No."

"Ready for more?"

"Actually, I'd like a nap." His face fell, and she bopped him lightly in the shoulder. "I'm kidding, Peter."

"Thank Christ!" He kissed her and she could taste herself, a novel and entirely exciting experience. She licked his lower lip and then sucked it into her mouth. She felt him take her hand and place it on him. Her fingers closed around his erection and she nearly shuddered with need. She'd never wanted anything in her life as much as she wanted the hot, hard, throbbing length that filled her hand so completely.

She tugged him toward her.

"Uh, Lori . . ."

"Do more," she ordered. He had been—it had been—and that was just the warm-up! She was wild for the main event, and anxious for his pleasure.

"You're not a virgin or anything, are you?"

She let go of his cock, not without regret, and stared up at him. His chest was heaving lightly as he panted, and she put her palms on the warm flesh. "No, I'm not a virgin."

He shifted under her touch, forcing her palms to touch his nipples. "You just seem sort of—uh—surprised."

"I am. You're the best lover I've ever had. Of course, there've only been two." She covered her mouth and giggled.

"Oh," he said, with evident relief. "OK. I just wanted to make sure—OK." He reached over, fumbled open the bedside drawer, and then she heard him tear open the condom packet.

"Let me do it," she said, sitting up. "I took a class."

"You're shitting me."

"I certainly am not. We used bananas. I got an A!"

"Lucky me."

She could hear the suppressed laughter in his voice and resisted the urge to bite him again.

"Why'd you take a class?"

She shrugged. "I thought if I learned more I'd enjoy it more." She pulled the condom out, tossed the foil packet in the general direction of the bedside table, and pressed the rolled disc to his glistening tip. Then slowly, while kissing his chest—and giving him a quick nip—she rolled it down to his lush nest of pubic hair. It took some time and care. He was enormous.

"Ahhhhh," he said, pulling her up for a deep kiss. "You've got the touch, all right." She felt him cup one of her breasts, testing the weight, and then he eased her back. "Lori, you're so beautiful. Not just your face and hair, but everything else, too. I can't believe no one ever told you what a knockout you are."

"I can't believe you're so good at this."

He bent to her and sucked a nipple into his mouth.

"Did *you* take a class?"

He laughed around her flesh. "No. Lost my virginity when I was twelve. That was a long time ago. Had some practice since then, I guess." He kissed her palm, then slipped his hands beneath her, squeezed her buttocks for a long moment, savoring her, then lifted her toward him. She spread her legs and arched toward him as he entered with excruciating care.

It was like—it was like being entered by something divine, something beyond her, and although he was the largest man she'd ever seen, she seemed to fit him perfectly. Before he was even all the way in, he was stroking shallowly, and she whimpered and instinctively wrapped her legs around him to force him closer.

"I want to feel you," she whispered in his ear. "Don't be careful."

He obliged and she felt him shove all the way home, then pull back and thrust again, hard enough to slam the headboard against the wall. She shrieked his name and met his thrust. For a while there was no sound but their harsh breathing and the headboard slamming against the wall. She felt his hands on her breasts, squeezing, felt his thumbs running across her nipples, and made fists and forced them to her sides.

"OK?" he panted.

"Yessssss. I'm afraid I'll scratch—"

"I don't mind, sweetie."

So she put her arms around him, and when he yanked her toward him at the exact moment of his thrust, she buried her nails in his shoulders.

"Uh-oh," he said, and was he laughing again? He was! "I'm close, darlin'. Thinking about baseball isn't going to cut it." He reached down and rubbed his thumb across her clit, so very lightly she could barely feel his touch, but that, combined with the sensation of being completely filled with his cock, was enough to send her spinning into another orgasm. She bucked against him, and then he stiffened and she saw his eyes roll up, and he collapsed over her.

"Holy shit," he groaned into her hair.

"Do more," she said sleepily, and he groaned again. "Later, I mean."

"How about next week? I ought to recover by then. You're a firecracker, Red."

"No, I'm not," she said seriously. She was stroking the

back of his neck. He was heavy, but it was a good weight, comforting. Not frightening at all. "I didn't do anything. You did most of the work."

"Umm. Yeah, it was a real hardship, touching that white, soft skin, and kissing that lush mouth of yours, going down on the sweetest-smelling pussy on the planet, and feeling your legs wrap around my back and your heels dig into my spine."

"Thank you," she replied politely, hoping he couldn't see her blush in the dark. She yawned, glanced at the clock . . . and had to look again. A quarter to four! They'd been at it for over an hour!

"Wow!"

"My thought exactly," he said, and rolled to his side, pulling her with him until they were cuddled together.

Chapter Eight

Peter opened his eyes and stared at the cobweb in the corner of the ceiling. Had to have been a dream. Had to. There was no way in hell a rich, classy dame like Lori would ask him to bed her. *No* way. A dream, for sure. The best wet dream of his life. The—

She turned in her sleep, and reddish-blond strands fell across his chest. Her face was pressed against his bicep and she snored lightly.

"Holy shit!" he said, and her eyes flew open. She sat up and he had a moment to admire the way the sunlight splashed against her breasts. Her nipples were bubble-gum pink. Yum.

"What? What?"

"Sorry. I had—never mind, it'll sound dumb."

"I'm sure it will, but you could tell me anyway," she said, then smirked at him.

He caught her gently by the hair and pulled her down to him. "Wiseass. How you feeling?"

"Wonderful." She stretched, her long body writhing against him in a most interesting way. "I'm so glad I forced you to come to bed with me."

He snorted. "Yeah, someone a foot shorter can always push me around."

"Well . . . I did, didn't I?" She rested her chin on his chest. "Did you really lose your virginity when you were twelve?"

"Sure. Only thing I was ever good at," he said truthfully.

"That's not true. You're good at—uh—" Her eyes went far-away as she tried to think of something.

"Thanks, Red. Never mind. How about you?"

"Oh, I'm good at lots of things," she assured him solemnly.

"Very funny. How old were you?"

"You'll laugh."

"Prob'ly."

"It was last year."

He did laugh, then grunted when she made a fist and smacked him in the ribs. "How old are you?"

"Twenty-five."

"Shit, you're a baby! I turned thirty-nine last year."

"So you're actually forty."

"Oh, shut up," he grumbled.

"Peter Random, vain about his age!" She clapped a hand over her mouth to stifle the giggle.

"You're gonna love coughing up a lung, you don't get off this."

She smiled at him. "Sure, tough guy."

"Why'd you wait so long?"

Her smile disappeared, and her eyes actually seemed to darken. "I had . . . some problems at home."

"With your stepfa—with your mother's husband?" He felt his hands lock into fists, and forced himself to unclench.

"No." She shook her head. "With his son. He was a couple years older than me, and I—I—" He saw with concern that the color was rapidly falling out of her face; she was almost the color of the sheets.

"Never mind. You don't have to go into all the gory details. Fought him off, didya?"

"My mom got home in time. And nothing happened after, for a long time. But I never felt safe in the house again, not if she was gone. And her hours—she was a doctor, y'know?

When I finally got up the courage to tell her what had happened—what had almost happened—she kicked him out of the house. But it took a while for her to catch on that her husband was just as bad as the son."

"He didn't try to stick up for his kid?"

"No. That would have gotten my mom's wind up. It would have ruined his plans."

He took her hand, which had curled into a fist of its own, gently opened it, and rubbed her palm where her fingernails had dug into the soft flesh. "I take it your mom was pretty happy to be married to this guy?"

"I couldn't wreck that for her. I—she was so lonely before, and we didn't know—she couldn't see how bad they were. I was home alone with them, and they thought I was stupid, so I saw, but I was weak, and—and—" Her chest began to hitch, but her expression never changed.

"Shit, Lori, you were a kid. That's too much to ask of anyone. A whiney, annoying kid, prob'ly, but a kid just the same."

She laughed unwillingly.

"And now you're getting the last laugh, right? Giving all that money away?" He groaned inwardly at the thought, but made sure none of it showed. He wasn't the only one in this bed with a poker face. "The money's probably the whole reason they came into your life in the first place. Right?"

Lori smirked, and a bit of color came back into her face. She pulled the sheet loose and flung it over her shoulders, like a cape. "You're right. You should have heard Ed hectoring my mother about the money all the time. After they'd been married a year or so, he started in on her." She bounded off the bed and marched back and forth, the sheet flapping behind her. "The money, the money, the money. He couldn't believe she wasn't spending it, had just dumped it in a trust for me. It was always, 'Lori's too young for the responsibility, let me help, at least make me the guardian of the trust,' blah-blah-blah."

"Well." He crossed his arms behind his head and enjoyed

the view. Lori looked like a naked superhero in his old sheet. "Let's go to your lawyer's office, get that checkbook, and spend some of it."

"All of it," she corrected.

"*Almost* all of it," he corrected back.

She scowled. "Fine, *fine.*" She wriggled in the sheet. "Gah, I'm all sticky from last night."

"Really?" he asked, interested. "Because I'm hard from this morning." He tugged her toward him. The sheet hit the floor, and his erection slapped his stomach. "See?"

"I could hardly miss it."

Trying to sound as hopeful as he felt, he asked, "Want to practice with condoms again?"

With a wicked grin, she held up a silver packet. He nearly fell off the bed in surprise. "Now, when did you grab *that?*"

"You just never mind."

She got the rubber on him in record time—so nice to know a girl with talents—and then pounced on him.

"Let's fly some more."

"What?"

"That's what it was like," she said stubbornly, anticipating his laugh. "Flying."

"Awww, you're so cute." He rolled her over until she was on her stomach, then caressed the fine globes of her excellent butt. He nudged her, forcing her up on her knees a bit, and stroked the damp curls between her legs. She was squirming against his hand, but when he slipped two fingers inside her, she went still as a rabbit, except for the occasional quiver.

He worked her until she was good and slick, marveling at how she felt, slippery and silky at once, and then spread her wide and slowly entered her. She backed up to meet him, and in less than a second he was fully seated within her, and biting back a groan.

"Flying," she whispered.

He put a hand in the middle of her back while he thrust, in

case she got more ideas about going anywhere, while he stroked her inner thighs with his other hand.

Lori was groaning into the pillow, her hips jerking against his, and he actually felt the temperature change when she popped off around him. Her silky walls gripped him with unbearable sweetness for a moment, and then he tipped over the edge and emptied himself into her.

He collapsed, breathing hard. Was the room naturally this dim, or was there something wrong with his eyes after that fine fuck?

"I really have to insist," Lori groaned, "that you get off me. I'm having trouble breathing."

"Picky picky," he replied, but did as she asked and rolled over on his back. "Now we both need a shower."

"Not to mention a nap. That was amazing. No one ever—I never felt like that before."

"Oh, I'm full of surprises."

"Yes, indeed." She laughed at him, and he chased her to the shower.

"I'll only be a moment," she said, already unbuckling her seat belt.

"I'm coming with you." He shut off the car and met her on the sidewalk. They were in one of the worst neighborhoods in St. Paul. He swore he could hear gunfire if he listened hard enough. Not that this bothered him. Made him kind of homesick, in fact.

"Jesus Christ!" he said, when she got all the locks undone and they stepped inside. "Who got beaten to death in here?"

"I haven't had much time to clean up," she said defensively.

"You live," he observed, stepping over a mound of laundry that twitched when he approached, "in a hole."

"Well." It was a one-room studio, and she was busy in the corner, pulling clothes out of her bureau and stuffing them into her gym bag. "I had to get away from my mother's husband, didn't I? D'you think he'd come looking for an heiress here? Besides, it's kind of fun, cooking for myself and doing my own laundry."

"I see no evidence of the latter. I guess it's a good plan, though. And if anyone did come looking for you here, they'd never be seen again. Eyecchh!"

"Oh, cut it out, you big baby."

"Hey, even I got standards, Red."

"More than you know," she muttered.

"What?"

"I said, time to go."

He let it drop, and broke several speed laws putting distance between her nasty apartment and the lawyer's office in Edina. He might have grown up in the Minneapolis version of Hell's Kitchen, but his mama would have beaten any germ that dared show its face in their home.

They pulled up outside the law offices of Gretch and Gretch—

"Don't start. He can't help his name."

—and he held the door open for her. She swept through like a runway model and flashed him a smile that he felt somewhere around his balls.

"Lori!"

The smile vanished and she actually swayed on her feet. He caught her elbow before she could do a nosedive into the tasteful gray carpet and spotted the guy pacing in the reception area. No receptionist; just a sign propped up on the computer that read, BE RIGHT BACK!

"Oh," Lori said faintly, and gently pulled her elbow out of Peter's grasp. "It's you. And I'm dumb enough to be surprised."

The guy stepped up, too far into Lori's space. He was at least a head taller and had at least sixty pounds on her, most of it football muscle going to flab. The thought of having this lug on top of Lori, trying to force her, was nightmarish. For the first time in forever, Peter had goose bumps. Or, in his case, pissed-off bumps.

He raised a finger. *Try to be nice. We're in a lawyer's office.* "Uh . . . buddy . . ."

"Cut all the shit, Lori. You know the money belongs to my dad."

Peter had this guy's number in about a nanosecond. Big, broody. Blond hair, piggy brown eyes. Solid, but the type who would go to fat within a decade. Thought PMS jokes were the height of wit. A real stud in high school, and only now waking up to the fact that being a big shot in school meant diddly shit in the real world. Waking up to it, and frightened of it. And lashing out at the most convenient targets.

Pound him, his inner voice whispered enthusiastically. *He's got it coming. This was the guy Lori was having a nightmare about! Blacken both those eyes and knock out half his teeth. It'll be fun. And a good deed!*

Peter cracked his knuckles and smiled in anticipation. Unlike most people, Peter had only a devil on his shoulder; his angel had packed up and hit the trail years ago.

"Peter, this is Conrad Burle," Lori was saying, ever the polite broad. "My mother's stepson."

"Meetcha, Burle," Peter grunted. Where first? Body work was good, and the grunts of pain would be satisfying, but maybe he should just break the guy's nose instead. A few shots to the ribs would be OK—he could crack one, and Burle-baby wouldn't sneeze without major pain until Easter. It was a buffet of felony assault!

"Conrad," he-who-would-soon-be-bleeding corrected peevishly.

"Huh?"

"It's just Conrad," Lori explained quietly.

"Like Madonna," Conrad added, sounding ridiculously proud. "Or Cher."

"Or asshole," Peter suggested. *Eh, Red would probably get pissed if I beat him up here, anyway. Plus, the lawyer's probably around here somewhere. Some other time. For sure.* "OK, Connie, now that we all know everyone's name, why don't you hit the bricks?"

Conrad pointed at Lori. "Not without her."

"Forget it." Lori, Peter saw, wasn't even looking at her

stepbrother. Just staring over his shoulder with cool disinterest. "Go away, Conrad. Go away now."

Conrad lunged forward and grabbed Lori's arm. "Damn it, Lori, I'm your husband!"

Peter was so startled, he forgot to break Conrad's wrist.

Chapter Nine

"You're her *what?*" Peter swung around and speared her with a furious glare. "Did we forget a few more details yesterday, Red?"

"He certainly is not my husband," she snapped. "Not legally. And you can just stop looking at me like that right this minute, Peter Random!"

He gaped at her. She supposed a man his size wasn't used to being yelled at. Too damned bad. She crossed her arms over her chest and glared. It was infinitely less nerve-racking than glaring at Conrad. She supposed it was hard to ever get over your childhood nightmares, no matter how ridiculous they became in maturity.

Peter's jaw, which had been unhinged, snapped closed. "He's not?"

Conrad, ever needing to be the center of attention, squeezed. Lori refused to let herself wince, though the feeling of her wrist bones grinding against each other was just short of excruciating. "Damn it, Lori, you're my wife. You know you are!"

How tiresome he was! Frightening—she knew his father was a high-functioning sociopath, and suspected his son might be one as well—but tiresome. "I didn't sign the marriage certificate, and you damned well know it." She turned to Peter.

"It was the last thing they tried, right before I disappeared. However, it's not legal without all the appropriate signatures. But they were desperate and assumed I was stupid."

"Compared to my dad, you are," Conrad muttered.

Lori ignored the interruption. "Besides, Conrad was always a sore loser, and not terribly bright. Also, he's still holding my arm."

"Boy," Peter said with frightening gentleness, "you've got three seconds to let go of the lady. One—two—"

"Aaaaaaauuuuuuuuggggggggghhhhhhhh!"

"Time goes kind of fast when I'm pissed off," he said cheerfully. "Bad Conrad! No touchie!"

Lori stared. Her childhood nemesis was rolling around on the floor cradling his forearm, which had an odd bulge in the middle.

"What's going on here?"

She turned to see Alan Gretch, her mother's lawyer and an old family friend, walking swiftly into the reception area. He stepped over the writhing Conrad—he knew him of old—and pulled her into an affectionate hug. "Lori! By God, you get prettier every week."

She extricated herself, blushing. "Thank you, Alan. This is my friend, Peter."

Peter scowled and stuck out a hand—the one he'd just broken Conrad's arm with. "Meetcha," he muttered. And, in a low voice to Lori, "Friend?"

"Oh, hush up. Would you prefer it if I drew him a diagram?"

"Do you need an ambulance?" Alan was crouching beside Conrad and speaking slowly, as if to an imbecile. Which in this case wasn't far off. Conrad's screams had died down to bubbly whimpers.

"Fuck you!" he gasped.

"So no?" Alan guessed.

"I'll help him outside," Peter offered. "He just needs some fresh air."

"And some plaster," Alan observed. "And possibly a sling."

Before Lori could protest—although she had no idea what she might have said—Peter had pulled Conrad off the floor by his good arm and accidentally walked him into the wall. Conrad howled and clapped his good hand over his eye. "Whoops! Missed the door by a few feet. Oh, and Conrad?" Peter's booming voice dropped to a whisper, and though she and Alan strained, they couldn't make out what Peter was saying. Conrad shuddered all over, then nodded so hard and fast he nearly reeled backward.

"What a nice young man," Alan commented.

"He's my—" What? Boyfriend? Too soon. Friend? Not after last night. Bad guy? Hard to tell. Savior? Getting there. "—he's very nice." Of course, that wasn't right, either.

Alan had taken her hand, and she blinked up at him in surprise. Not too far up—Alan only had about three inches on her. He was a kind man, a clever attorney, and had made no secret of the fact that he'd harbored a not-so-secret crush on her for two years.

It's funny, Lori thought, taking in his silvery blond hair, the friendly brown eyes bracketed with laugh lines, the hopeful smile, the expensive suit. *He's twenty years older than me—practically a father figure—and I could have taken him ages ago. He would have solved all my problems. Why not? Was I really waiting for someone like Peter all this time?*

Not someone like *Peter . . . was I really waiting for Peter himself?*

Ridiculous. We have nothing in common, she thought, still gazing up at Alan. *Peter thinks I'm a basket case and I think he's a thug, and the fact that we're both right doesn't help matters. Not one bit.*

"I'm sorry, Alan, I wasn't paying attention. What did you say?"

"I said I've got the paperwork and the trust checkbook right here, but I was really just screwing up my courage."

"Beg your pardon?"

He took a deep breath. "I adore you, Lori, and I want to be with you. I've never met anyone like you. I've just been waiting for you to grow up. I want you to be my wife."

"Oh," she said weakly.

"I'm sorry. This is a horrible time and place to propose—"

"Oh?"

"—I had it planned all different, you know, with dinner and nice flowers and violins and things, but seeing you here with someone else—I just had to do it right now. Before another minute went by. I've already waited so long, you know."

"Oh." Two days ago she'd thought she was all alone. Now she was—er—involved with Peter, and a respected lawyer wanted her hand in marriage. And Conrad was on his way to the ER. And she had to spend close to a million dollars in the next day or two. "Ah—oh."

"And it's not about the money!" he said urgently, although for once the money was the farthest thing from her mind. "I have plenty of my own. I just—I couldn't wait. You understand, don't you, Lori?" he pleaded.

"Of course. I'm—I'm flattered, Alan, but surprised. And I don't—"

"Don't answer yet," he begged.

He had inadvertently increased the pressure on her hand—the one Conrad had been mangling—and she hoped he'd let go before she had to ask him to. Her fingers were going numb, one by one.

"Just promise you'll think about it."

She couldn't bear to wipe the hope from his eyes. She knew exactly how it felt, having your dreams dashed. It was the worst. "I promise," she said.

Life, she thought as he handed her the trust checkbook, was certainly getting interesting. For once, in a good way.

Chapter Ten

You fuckin' moron.

He only had himself to blame. He'd been right all along—a rich, classy dame like Lori wouldn't stick with him in the long run, even if she did live in a dump and needed a housekeeper in a major way. She was using him to get what she needed, and then it was sayonara, Jack.

He wasn't mad at her. Much. He was mad at himself, for thinking for two seconds . . .

Never mind. He should have learned. He *had* learned. Everyone was out for themselves. The Jackal, Renee, Lori, that lawyer dude, Conrad, and probably Lori's dead mother.

Serves you right for eavesdropping.

Well, like Rhett told Scarlett in *Gone with the Wind*—probably the best movie of the last century—eavesdroppers often heard highly interesting things.

They spent the afternoon writing checks. Well, she did. He played Personal Driver. They stopped at AirLifeLine, the Minnesota Valley Humane Society, Bridging, Inc., Meals on Wheels, and the Children's Safety Center Network.

With every check she wrote, he could see Lori get happier and happier, see her spirits lift and her load lighten, practically before his eyes. It was amazing, if weird. *Jeez, this money really is a burden to her. She can't wait to get rid of it.*

"—really make a difference, I just wish my mom could see what we're doing with Grandpa's money, she'd be so—"

"You oughta give some to ProofCorp," he muttered.

She quit in mid babble and looked at him with her pretty gray eyes. "What's ProofCorp?"

"It's this company that donates bulletproof vests to police precincts."

"Oh. Don't the police provide—"

"Suckers are expensive," he grunted, turning the wheel and heading back to his place. It was the end of a long, long day. "Not all the departments can afford them, or if they can, they can't buy as many as they need."

"How do you know so much about it?" she asked.

"I just do, is all."

"Come on, Peter."

No way was he telling her his dream, the reason he played the lottery every week. Not when she was set to piss away all her money and marry Retch-the-lawyer.

He shrugged.

"Fine, don't tell me." She crossed one shapely leg over the other and jiggled her foot up and down. "It's a good idea, though. Maybe we can head back to your place—oh. Here we are. Well, good. I thought we could get a bite and rest, and spend the rest of the money tomorrow. Sound good?"

He grunted.

"Are you all right?"

He muttered.

She was clearly puzzled as she followed him up the walk, but she didn't say anything. Good thing, because he was in no mood.

He stopped suddenly, and she ran smack into him.

"Oof!"

"Agghh! I mean, Mrs. O'Halloran, how ya doin'?"

"There you are, you bad boy. And where's my rent, now?"

Lori peeked around him. Peter was sure Lori figured Mrs. O'Halloran looked like a harmless TV sitcom grandma—curly white hair, glasses, plump figure, faded jeans and a denim workshirt. What Red couldn't know was that his landlady was really a hydra in disguise.

"Hello," she said, sticking out her hand. "My name's Lori."

"Betty O'Halloran. Nice to meet you, dear."

"Uh, about the rent—"

Lori was scribbling in the trust checkbook. It really was like a book; it was about a foot long and eight inches wide. She had to bend over and rest it against her thighs to balance it. He put out a hand to stop her, when O'Halloran broke his train of thought.

"Now, Peter, dear, I know you're out of work. You can just get me the rent when you're back on your feet again. Don't you worry about a thing."

"You take that back!" he practically shouted. "I know you, you've probably been showing the house while I was out."

"Only to six or seven families," she said, having the gall to sound wounded. "I've got to look out for myself, dear. An old woman living on a pension . . ."

"You bought IBM stock in 1984!" he howled. "My house is one of twenty-four!"

"Here," Lori said, cutting him off and handing O'Halloran a check. "This should take care of it."

O'Halloran glanced at the small piece of paper and her eyes went shiny, the way they always did when she contemplated money—or wounded animals. "Ah—yes, this will do it. Thank you."

"That's all right," Lori said comfortably, and waved when Mrs. O'Halloran hotfooted it across the street.

"She's probably going to hitch up her broom and head straight to the bank," he mumbled.

"I heard that, dear!"

Peter yanked his screen door open and fished for his front door key. "You didn't have to do that," he said irritably. Yeah, so, Red saved his ass—not to mention his home—but damned if he liked being beholden to her.

"Why not? I owe you a salary, anyway. You're working for

me, remember?" She grinned. "Six months' rent seemed like a good starting point. Besides, there's not that much money left in the account, thank God."

"And the stud service? What's that worth?"

She almost walked into the door frame. "What's that supposed to mean?"

"You need hand puppets?"

Shocked, she stared at him. Then she shot out of his line of sight and the left side of his face went numb.

She slapped me!

"Never," she whispered. "Never ever. Imply that. Ever again."

"Ouch!" He balled a fist, then let it drop to his side. Who was he kidding? He'd never hit a woman in his life. He certainly wasn't going to start with Red. "Don't do that again," he said through gritted teeth. The gal packed quite a punch. He ran his tongue across his teeth—yes, everything seemed to be in place. "You won't like the consequences."

"Blow me," she snapped.

He blinked at her, but before he could answer, his front door opened and a hand shot out, seized him by the hair, and dragged him inside.

Chapter Eleven

"Ow, goddamn it!"

"Boy, you got what you deserved, and if I hear you talking to a lady like that again, you'll get a whole lot worse."

His face throbbed. His skull was on fire. His eyes were watering. What vicious beast had waylaid him in his own home? He wrenched himself away. "Mama! Cut that out! And how'd you get in here, anyway?"

"Don't ask stupid questions, boy. Your landlady let me in."

"Remind me to shoot her," he grumped.

"Hello," Lori said tentatively, shutting the front door and holding out her hand. "My name's Lori. You must be Mrs. Chuck."

"Darling, you call me Mama, all right? Yes. My, you're a beautiful little thing, aren't you!" Since Lori had about six inches on Mama, "little" was a bit ludicrous.

"Thank you. Peter's been helping me out this week."

"Oh, I'm sure," Mama Chuck said. She tried a leer, but it looked like an attack of indigestion. She was an emaciated woman with skin so dark it had mahogany undertones. Her wrists were little over an inch across. Her eyes were, interestingly, the color of apple cider. Her hair, streaked with white, was pulled back tightly and fastened in a bun low on her neck. She was wearing cocoa-colored leggings, a faded sweatshirt, and knee-high red rubber boots. Her face was remarkably un-lined. She could have been thirty-five or sixty-five.

"Jeez, Mama, you still losing weight? What about that case of Ensure I brought over?"

"Tastes like chalk," she said shortly. "Chocolate-flavored chalk."

"I don't give a fuck if it tastes like hot piss, drink it. Keep your weight on—ow!"

She'd smacked him in the back of the head, *Three Stooges*–style. "Watch your mouth, Peter Neville Random. And you've got some explaining to do."

"Neville?" Lori asked.

"Like hell!" he shouted, backing out of her reach. "Mama, I'm a grown man, you can't—"

"Neville?"

"Randall and his boys ran into you at the MegaMall with this little cutie, and you didn't say a word. You didn't call me over, and you sure didn't bring her to visit. I got to hear about your doings from my own boys?"

"You act like it's a real rare thing when I've been in the company of a woman," he whined.

"Oh, Neville?" Lori was grinning. He refused to look at her.

There was a short, pointed silence, broken by Mama Chuck tapping her teeny, size-four triple-A foot. Peter could feel his face getting red. "OK, still," he mumbled. "Grown man. Mind your own business. Stop bugging me. Go away now."

"Neville and I have only known each other for a day or two," Lori added, coming to his rescue. Thank you, Jesus! "He's helping me out of a bit of a jam. There really hasn't been time for niceties."

"Peter never makes time for niceties," Mama said. "Sweetie, you want to excuse us for a minute? I need to kick this boy's ass up and down the living room, and you shouldn't have to watch."

Lori eyed the tiny, energetic woman and the hulking Peter, who was actually shuffling his feet, and made a graceful exit to the bedroom. He watched her go, he couldn't help it, even though he knew Mama wouldn't miss a trick.

"What's the matter, sweetie?"

"Nothing. I got a new job."

"Uh-huh. Randall said you could hardly take your eyes off her at the Mall. What you waiting for?"

"Forget it, Mama. She's different from us. Rich, classy, white . . ."

"I hate to break this to you again," Mama said dryly, "but you're white."

"You know what I mean. She's living in a dump right now, but she grew up in a mansion. She's pissing away close to a million bucks, and you should see her with this money—she can't *wait* to get rid of it."

"So? Then she'll be in your league."

"No chance." He kicked at his carpet. "Besides, she's going to marry some jerkoff lawyer."

"If you let that happen, you're the jerkoff," his mama said sternly. Peter raised his eyebrows in surprise. That was pretty profane, for his mother. "Fix it so it doesn't happen. Win her over. Don't just let her walk away from you. Peter, if she means this much to you, don't be a fool. Not about this."

"What's *that* supposed to mean?"

"You're really good at letting happiness slip through your fingers," she said simply. "Haven't I known you since you were toilet-trained? Didn't I take you in when that worthless father of yours started using you for batting practice? Haven't I seen it? Not this time, Peter. She needs someone; I knew that the second I saw her. Why can't it be you?"

"You don't know anything about her," he replied. "So how can you know we'll be good together?"

"I'm your mama. I know *everything*."

He shrugged and stared at the floor. "Don't think it's gonna be that easy."

"Try first," she said tartly. *"Then* you can give up. Do what you're good at, boy. Get her between the sheets and show her how you feel. What woman could resist you?"

"Don't talk like that," he said, revolted. He preferred to assume his mother was a virgin. Hey, it was possible—he was adopted, after all.

"Everybody's good at something," she said slyly. "Some more than others—or so I hear."

"Seriously. Mama. I'm going to puke, you don't cut that out."

There was a knock on the door, and Mama turned. "I'll get it. You think about what I said. You were always bright, but you sometimes act like a fool."

"Thanks," he said sarcastically.

"Well, you do," she snapped, peeking through the peephole. "Huh. Some rich-looking white man. Nice suit."

"Probably the lawyer. Let him in."

"Why?" she asked scornfully, then swung the door open.

An imposing man stood in the doorway. Mama Chuck was right; his black suit was beautifully cut and fit him perfectly. He looked down his long nose at them. Though he was nearly Peter's height, he was at least forty pounds lighter. His hands were beautiful—long, thin fingers, clearly manicured. His eyes were the color of frozen mud. His hair was pure white. He looked like a prosperous mortician.

"I'm seeking my stepdaughter and the trust checkbook," he said coolly, not even glancing at Mama. "You'll will deliver both, at once."

Chapter Twelve

Lori heard the voice and nearly fell down. She knew it well. Hadn't it spoken to her, taunted her, hurt her in enough nightmares?

Edward! Edward's out there with Peter and Mama Chuck!

She shoved the remarkably ugly cat off her lap and sprinted through the bedroom doorway. "You leave them alone!" she shrieked, skidding to a halt in front of Edward and nearly knocking Mama into the DVD collection.

His cool gaze fell on her like a weight. "Ah, Lori, there you are. I was just explaining to your . . . friends . . . that you'll be coming with me. And you'll bring the checkbook, of course."

"My ass," Lori blurted, and took courage from the way Mama Chuck lifted a hand to cover the sudden smile. "Get out of here, Edward. You're not in my family anymore, and I'm not a child. I don't have to listen to you or cover up for you or do what you tell me *ever again.*"

"Also," Peter added, "you're an asshole."

"Get out of here," Lori thundered. Well, squeaked.

"Gladly. You'll be coming with me, of course. Unless you want your friend arrested for assault. Conrad's arm is broken in two places. You shouldn't have set your guard dog on my son, girly. I wasn't sure what lever to use until you did that."

"Poor Connie's arm hurts? Awwwwwww," Peter said, not

looking too worried about police intervention. Lori noticed that everything was happening so fast, he hadn't had time to take off his greatcoat, the one that made him look like a bear. "Pardon me while I cry a fucking river."

"Go ahead," she said. "Have him arrested!"

"Thanks, babe," Peter said dryly.

"I'll testify for him! I'll tell the police *everything*. And I'll pass a lie detector test, too, you *know* I will. How about your son going up on charges of attempted rape? How about you facing the music for attempted embezzlement? And you can face assault charges yourself!"

"Don't be a fool."

Oh, she wanted to kill him. "Did you really think I believed my mother when she said she ran into the door? Six times in two weeks? You're not as clever as you think. Conrad was gone by then, but you were still after her about the money. The fucking money. But she died, she got away from you. And—and—"

"You smacked Red's mom around?" Peter asked with deceptive calm.

"Here!" Lori shrilled. She had grabbed the trust checkbook on her way out of the bedroom, and now threw it at Edward's head. He moved, showcasing the quickness that had always terrified her as a child, and caught it. His cold smile faded as she continued, "It's all gone, anyway! I've been spending the money since this morning! The last check was for Mama Chuck, and I just dare you to try and take it away from her!"

"Yeah," said Mama Chuck. Then, "What?"

"It's over, Eddie," Peter said. "Lori's not going with you, Connie's just gonna have to find some other broad to make miserable. And the money's kaput. Gone. I was there—she spent it left and right. It was pretty funny. Weird, though," he added under his breath.

"Get lost, swineherd," Mama Chuck said. "Or I'll send some of my kids around to see how many of your bones they can break before they get tired."

"You could have been happy," Lori said quietly. Her wild

hysteria had died, leaving a kind of awful calm. She was having trouble processing what was happening. She was standing up to the devil, and Peter and Mama Chuck were helping. "But you'll always be bent, always need more than people can give you. All you've got is Conrad, and he'll drop you in a heartbeat for a big enough paycheck."

"Don't let the door hit you in the ass on the way out," Peter added cheerfully.

"Good-bye, you frog-faced troglodyte."

"Troglodyte?" Ed looked at Mama Chuck with distaste.

"Master's in literature," Peter explained.

"How interesting. I'll leave when I wish, thank you," Edward said. He paged through the checkbook and eyed the register, which was down to sixty-seven dollars and eighty-four cents. "I hardly need to take direction from a thug, a whore, and a nigger midget,"

"That's *Doctor* Nigger Midget," Mama Chuck snapped.

"Doctorate in English," Peter supplied helpfully.

"Don't you talk to them like that," Lori said, trembling. Whore? Had he really called her that? She was sure most whores had more experience than she did.

"Call the cops if you want," Peter said, moving forward and seizing Edward by the elbow. "But be ready to answer some questions if you do. And don't worry about stopping payment on the checks—you aren't authorized. Only Lori can do that, and I'm not letting you or the asshole you raised within five feet of her. Starting now."

Edward's feet actually left the floor as Peter propelled him out the front door. "Get your hands off me, you Neanderthal!"

"All in good time, Captain Psycho," Peter soothed. "Also, come near Lori again and I'll kick your ass up so high, people will think you have a second head. Which reminds me . . . about Lori's mom . . ."

Edward had time to fix Lori with a baleful look before the door slammed.

Lori let out a shaky breath. "Wow." Then she cocked her

head. Very faintly, through the door, she could hear a muffled thud, and then . . . retching?

"Gut punch," Mama Chuck said.

"I—I'm going to be a doctor, too," Lori said.

Mama Chuck smiled. "We have a lot in common." She nodded toward the door, where they could hear Peter smacking Edward around. "More than you might think."

As soon as Mama Chuck left, Lori jumped into Peter's arms. She couldn't help it. She felt like a weight—a hundred-ninety-pound, six-foot-four weight—had been lifted from her shoulders.

Peter kissed her, hard, then lifted her, cupping his hands beneath her thighs, pressing her to him.

"It's over, I can't believe it," she was saying into his mouth, pulling at his overcoat. When he shrugged it off, she started on his shirt.

"One more time, then," he muttered, "just to remember you by," whatever the hell *that* meant, and then he was pulling at his clothes and yanking at her own, and in minutes they were nude and he was sitting down on the couch, holding her in his lap. She felt like a doll nestled against his big frame, and it was just fine.

She rained kisses on his face, his mouth, his throat, and he stroked her back and buttocks. She reached for his cock, which was stiff and throbbing, its tip bright red.

"Wait," he gasped. "I need to get a—"

"Not this time." She got both hands around it and squeezed, and he groaned into her hair. She shifted her weight and slowly impaled herself on him.

"Lori—too soon for you—"

"Hush up." It was tight, but the friction was delightful. The friction was *unbelievable*. Inch by inch he slipped up into her, until he was seated completely within and she could feel his thighs trembling.

"Oh," she sighed. "That's . . . that's really nice. I like that you're so big. I didn't think I would, you know."

He put a hand on the back of her neck and shifted his weight, and she felt a gush of wetness and had to swallow a gasp. Then he gripped her ass and began to pump while he sucked on the hollow of her throat. She thrust back, riding him, and the slippery sliding was exquisite, wasn't to be believed, and she hoped it would never, never end.

He reached down and rubbed a thumb across her clitoris and she bit his ear, hard. They writhed together and when she felt her uterus tighten in orgasm, she saw his eyes roll back in response to her body's urging.

They collapsed against each other, panting lightly. She shifted her weight and he slid out of her, and she curled up on the couch. She waited for him to come to her, but he remained sitting on the edge, his head in his hands.

"You can stay as long as you like," he said hollowly. "Just—give me a little notice when you decide to leave."

She yawned. "You *have* seen where I live, right? Why would I go back?"

"Cut the shit, Lori. I know what's going on."

"Doubtful. Tell the truth—that ugly cat that's around here somewhere? It's not a stray, is it? It's your pet."

Long silence, followed by, "Yeah."

"That's what I thought. I went looking for a tough guy, and I ended up with a pair of pussycats. It's just as well."

"What's your point, Lori?" Still he wouldn't look at her. Very strange!

"I'm in love with you," she said simply. "I want to stay. I'm poor now, but you'll have to overlook that and love me anyway."

He raised his head and stared at her with burning eyes. "You're marrying Retch."

"Is *that* what this is about? Why you've been acting like a cold jackass?"

"I have not. Hey, no big," he added quickly. "I knew you were just a temporary stop and all."

"Oh, really?"

"Yeah. Story of my life. Broads come, broads go."

"Well, you're stuck with this broad, you big moron." She crawled forward and nuzzled the crisp mat of hair between his nipples. "Peter, didn't you know? I adore you. I want to stay with you forever."

"Well, how the hell would I know that?" he said, sounding upset. "You never said!"

"I'm sorry," she soothed. "Of course. But I do, you know. That's why I called Alan and turned him down."

He straightened up so suddenly, she nearly fell off the couch. He caught her by the elbow and steadied her. "When did you do *that?*"

"While I was at AirLifeLine and you were sulking in the parking lot. After I wrote them a humongous check, they were happy enough to let me use the phone."

"Wasn't sulking. I just didn't think you should have dropped ninety grand so people can take free plane rides," he grumbled. "But get back to what you were saying—so you told Retch to fuck off?"

"I certainly did not. And his name is Gretch. I just turned him down nicely. I had no business equivocating in the first place," she added frankly. "But I had a lot on my mind at the time."

"I'll say," he said cheerfully, his mood appearing to improve by a factor of a thousand percent. "So you're not gonna marry the ambulance chaser?"

"No," she sighed. "Please don't call him that."

"Yeah, yeah. Then you can marry me."

"Is that a proposal?"

"No, it's a dare. And a proposal. What do you want, me on my knees with a damn ring?"

She said nothing. He groaned, and slid off the couch onto his knees. "Red, be my wife."

"It still sounds like an order. And it's *Lori,* damn it, do I have to paint it on my goddamned forehead?"

He laughed. "You are so cute when you swear! And paint it if you like. Besides, you think you got a choice? You were mine the second you conked out in the back of my car. And we're both poor. Now that you pissed away all the money, I'm out of a job again. I can't believe I'm marrying someone who gave her fortune away. I must be out of my fucking mind."

"So romantic," she said, her lips curving into a smirk. Peter promptly grabbed her knees and kissed them. "Ah, and now the besotted groom-to-be gives way to passion."

"No, I did that twenty minutes ago. Hey, shit, I gotta tell Mama Chuck! She's been on my ass to get married for ten years."

"Wait until she finds the check I slipped into her purse," Lori giggled. "She'll flip."

"You didn't have to do that," he said seriously. He picked her up and carried her back to the bedroom. "I take care of her."

"So? This way she can keep taking in stray children. Or she can retire to Maui. Whatever she wants. I owed her a big debt, anyway. For taking care of you. For saving you for me. But now you have to do something for me."

"What?"

"Tell me the secret you wouldn't tell me this afternoon. Why you know so much about what bulletproof vests cost."

"Well . . ." He placed her carefully in the center of the bed, then climbed in beside her. "It's kind of—well, there's this thing I always wanted to do for a living. Don't laugh."

She promised.

And he told her.

And she didn't laugh.

Chapter Thirteen

"You really play the lottery every week?"

"Yup. Gotta fund the dream somehow, and you gave all your money away."

"Worth it," she said fervently. She smiled as Mark, the bartender, refilled her glass. "We haven't heard from Conrad and Edward . . . proof! Proof that it was worth it. Um, is that why you wanted to know my birthday?"

"Well, playing Mama Chuck's birthday hasn't done shit," he grumped. Then, to Mark, "Do *not* give me a damned ginger ale. Still in law school?"

"I haven't dropped out in the last week, if that's what you're asking. And before you bug me again, we're still not hiring."

While Peter and Mark fell into an argument about why he should quit law school and open his own bar, she reached into his pocket and pulled out the lottery ticket.

Ridiculous. This little piece of paper was conceivably worth eight-point-two million dollars. It was amazing anybody played the lottery. The odds were—

She stared up at the television, then back down at the ticket.

"—world's got enough goddamned lawyers, but not nearly enough good bartenders—"

"Oh, sure, my life's goal is to pour booze for reprobates like you."

"Uh . . . Peter?"

"I'm just saying."

"And I'm just blowing you off."

"Peter? Are you watching this?"

"There are *some* good lawyers in the world."

"I've never met one."

"Well, after I pass the bar, you won't be able to say that anymore."

She thumped him on the shoulder. "Peter!"

"What?" He looked at her, took in her expression at a glance, then glanced up at the television. His jaw dropped. "Holy God!"

"Just when I got rid of all that money," she said faintly, and would have slid off the bar stood if he hadn't caught her. "Now I'm rich again, damn it."

Epilogue

NEW LOCAL COMPANY HAS BULLETPROOF IDEALS

St. Paul, Minnesota—Most lottery winners retire and live on their earnings for the rest of their lives. Not so Peter and Lori Random of St. Paul, Minnesota. The newlyweds have opened a non-profit agency, Random Acts, which makes, tests, and distributes bulletproof vests. Random Acts, which began with an inflow of lottery winnings, also accepts donations and counts among its sponsors Toro, Northwest Airlines, and US Bank.

"It was a little tricky in the beginning," explains Lori Random, who is expecting the couple's first child in July, and who manages day-to-day operations for Random Acts. "But Peter was determined to make it happen. We had a lot of help from the neighborhood kids, too. They're always volunteering their time."

When asked where he got the idea to start such a business, Peter Random replied, "What, you kid-

ding? I get to shoot guns all day for a living and test grown-up toys. What's not to love?"

Random Acts has already distributed close to a thousand bulletproof vests to local police precincts. Plans to expand to the East Coast are currently under way.

DELIGHTFUL DECEPTION

Chapter One

Thea Foster, MD, PhD, MBBS, and—this one had been for fun—PharmD, was a woman with a mission. Specifically, her mission was twofold: a) avoid termination, and b) avoid boredom. She was very much afraid that if she accomplished the first, the second was inevitable.

She pressed her thumb to the ID plate, waited a moment to be scanned, then stood by as the door to BioSecurity slid open. "Good morning, Dr. Foster," the computer husked, and she nearly grinned. Those fools in IT had been fooling around with Central's voice programming again. How else to explain why she had just been greeted by Marilyn Monroe's breathy contralto?

"Good morning, Central. Any schedule changes I should be aware of?" Probably not; as head of BioSecurity, there were precious few changes that were not immediately brought to her attention.

"No, Dr. Foster. I downloaded the new CEO's presentation into your Palm last night; nothing has changed."

Thea felt her mouth turn down in a grimace. The new CEO. Right. Not that she had forgotten—she had a photographic memory and it was, unfortunately, impossible for her to forget anything—but she'd shoved it to the back of her brain for a while.

After last quarter's debacle with the theft—OK, the dona-
tion—of PaceIC, the company's bottom line had gone well
over into red, with no hope in sight.

There were other eggs in Anodyne's basket, of course, but
nothing near completion. PaceIC had been their shot, and now
it was gone. Well, not entirely gone, but now there was market
competition, and their profit margin had been considerably
narrowed.

Thanks to me.

Well, yes. Thea hadn't liked the idea of making the suffer-
ing pay through the nose for *her* invention, thanks very much.
She had expressed this thought to Nicholas Jekell, aka the
Jackal. The Jackal had told her that as an employee of Anodyne,
anything she invented was the company's property, what they
did with it was none of her damned business, and if she didn't
like it, she could shove it up her frozen ass.

Forty-eight hours later, the head of security had left for the
day, completely unaware that she was carrying a vial worth
billions. Dr. Jekell never pieced it together—not all of it. For
once her IQ rep had been the saving of her. No one had considered for even a nanosecond that Dr. Foster had jettisoned
PaceIC . . . to be *nice*.

Motivated partly by altruism, but mostly by vengeance,
Thea had been shocked at how much she had enjoyed the
great good fun that had resulted. The ensuing chaos had been
the most interesting thing to happen in years, and if Renee had
had a rough time of it at first, things had turned out all right
for her in the end. Thea soothed her mildly guilty conscience—
pricked by the memory of gunshots and police intervention—
by recalling the proof in her briefcase: The wedding invitation
had come yesterday. She had no idea why Renee and what's-
his-name had invited her, but she meant to go. She was so
rarely invited anywhere.

Now the fun was done, unfortunately, and it was time to,
as her metaphor-mixing grandmother would say, face the
piper. Anodyne had been bought ought by wunderkind Jimmy

Scrye, who was coming this morning, doubtless to lay waste to personnel.

Well, it would be interesting, if nothing else.

Thea strode down the hallway, paused to deposit her briefcase in her office, and then headed for the lab. The door's electric eye scanned her and, reading the correct biosignature, obligingly opened.

Her staff was clustered around the play computer like a knot of lemmings trying to decide when to jump. They looked up at her, and she saw a blur of anxious expressions.

"Good morning," Thea said.

"Hi, boss."

"Morning, chief."

"Have you heard anything?" That last from her wide-eyed protégé, Jessica Lorentz. Jessica had been working for Anodyne for eighteen months and had been out of graduate school for eighteen and a half. Right now her blue eyes were quite round with distress, and her reddish brown curls were in wild disarray. She looked like a harassed Orphan Annie. "About the new owner?"

"Just that he's meeting with all the teams today. He's due here in another five minutes, so you might consider looking as though you are working instead of researching him on the Internet."

As one, the group straightened and backed away from the computer, which was used strictly for games, Internet searches, eBay bids, and online gambling. Thea pushed her team hard, and if they wanted to take a break and play a little blackjack, who was she to argue?

"There's not much to work on," Jack, one of her techs, pointed out. "I mean, with PaceIC gone, we don't have anything near ready—"

"I know."

Jessica elbowed Jack in the ribs. "Duh, she knows."

"Perhaps Dr. Scrye will give us some direction," Thea suggested.

"You ever had the big boss be younger than you?" Jack asked.

"In this field?" Thea smiled. "Frequently." And it was true. Her team leader at BioSine had been twenty-four, with a managing budget of two-point-two million. At thirty-three, Thea was an old lady. "I'm not worried about that. I'm worried about—"

She cut herself off. No need to give the team more to fret about.

"You *must* be worried," Jessica teased. "I don't think you've ever used the word, much less felt the emotion. Our IQ."

Only Jessica could get away with the Ice Queen thing, though others had tried. Thea was well aware that she came across as aloof. OK, cold. OK, frozen like Antarctica during a rough winter. She gave not a rat's ass. Results were what counted. If people called her IQ behind her back, that was fine. The important thing was that the work got done and into the field, to maximize aid.

Not Anodyne's bottom line, though the former CEO had disagreed with her on that one. And where was he now? Facing charges of conspiracy to kidnap, among other things.

It was almost enough to make her grin. Twice in one day!

"Well, what did you find out about our new fearless leader?" Thea asked, pretending she hadn't been up until 3:30 A.M. researching the hell out of Scrye.

Her team chimed in with answers, but nothing new: Born in Southern Pines, North Carolina. Orphaned at sixteen via a house fire, got his MD at nineteen after only three years, started his first biofirm at twenty-two, sold it for billions at twenty-five, made a practice of rescuing ailing biotech firms and turning them around. Today was his twenty-ninth birthday.

"Maybe he'll fire us all as a b-day present to himself," Marshall said gloomily.

Thea scowled at him over the tops of her glasses. "None of that, Miss Marshall."

As always, her cross-dressing research tech brightened when she referred to him in the feminine tense. "Sorry, Dr. Foster." Marshall fiddled with his pearls. "It's just—OK, I get that our shares are pretty much in the toilet now, but I really like this job. I wasn't here to get rich and move on . . . I *like* it here, OK? I wanted to stay and do stuff. I don't want to be looking for work. I mean, jeez . . ." Now he was actually nibbling on the necklace in his agitation. "You're the only boss I've ever had who lets me dress up for work."

"I'm sure it won't come to anything like that," she said automatically, but of course she was in no way certain. Scrye could fire them all and start over. Or he could fire half of them and rebuild the other half. Or he could leave things as they were. It was anyone's guess. And her research hadn't helped her formulate a plan, which was frustrating. What would a twenty-nine-year-old former prodigy *do* with them? "I think the best thing to do is—"

"Happ . . . eee birth . . . day . . . to . . . youuuuuuuu . . . happ . . . eee birth . . . day . . . to . . . youuuuuuuuuu . . ."

Thea covered her eyes. "Oh, dear God."

"Happ . . . eee *birth*dayyyyyyyy . . . Missster Pres . . . ih . . . dent . . ."

"Jeez, I forgot about Central being Marilyn today," Jack said innocently, which was an utter lie, as his cousin was the head of the IT department.

The door slid open, and a tall, balding man entered. He was dressed, surprisingly, in a sober black suit, with a light blue shirt and a blue bow tie with white polka dots. He looked more like a librarian than a hip young doctor.

He stared at them through his gold wire rims and waited patiently for the computer to stop serenading him.

". . . tooooooo . . . youuuuuuuuuuuuu. M-wah!"

"Did the computer just blow me an air kiss?" the man asked pleasantly.

"Uh—" was as far as Thea got. As God was her witness, she had no idea what to say.

Marshall sidled up to her. "I don't think that's the new boss," he whispered to her. "Unless he's aged ten years in two days."

"After the nonsense here, I may well have," whoever-it-was said dryly. "As it happens, my name is Don DePalma. James is—" He was interrupted by a blare of music, and sighed. "On his way."

It took Thea a moment to place the music. It was the theme from *Superman*.

James Edward Scrye II burst into the room. He was bizarrely arrayed in khaki shorts—in January!—a red button-down shirt, no socks, and red tennis shoes with yellow laces. She had a blurred impression of dark red hair and freckles, and then he was clambering atop one of the lab tables.

Oh, and the cape. She hadn't noticed the cape right away. It, too, was red, and Mr. DePalma stepped behind Scrye, grasped the hem of the cape, and flapped it gently as if Scrye were flying.

Meanwhile, the music blared on: "Daaaaah dah dih duh dah, *daaaaah, daaaaah, daaaaah*. Daaaah dah dih duh dah . . . *dah* duh *daah!*"

"People of Anodyne, hear me!" Scrye boomed. He had a surprisingly deep voice for a bio-nerd. "The forces of evil have been utterly defeated. I, Jimmy Scrye, have taken over this nest of evil-doers and from here on out, y'all are firmly on the side of good. Hear that? Repeat after me, please—"

"—dah dih duh dah, *daaaaah, daaaaah, daaaaah*. Daaaah dah dih duh dah—"

"—I will use my powers for good."

Stunned silence from Thea and her team.

"Say it," he threatened, "or I'll turn the music up."

"I will use my powers for good," they parroted.

"All righty then," he said, and leaped nimbly from the table. "Uh, Don, you can shut that off."

Mr. DePalma leaned over and pressed a button on the small boom box no one had seen him bring in.

"Okey-dokey then," Scrye said. He was bouncing back and

forth on the balls of his feet. His eyes were very green, the color of spring grass. He looked like he'd be carded to buy cigarettes. Heck, drain cleaner. But his quickness only exaggerated his feline grace, and she noticed his legs were ropy with muscle. "Which one of y'all is Dr. Foster?"

"I am," Thea said. She was trying very hard not to stare, and failing. "This is my primary team: Jessica, Marshall, and Jack."

"Right. You guys are the ones who thought up PaceIC."

"That was Dr. Foster," Jess, Marshall, and Jack said at once.

"It was a team effort," Thea said quietly.

"Bullshit. Sorry, Dr. Foster, but you know that's not true," Marshall said. He stomped his high-heeled foot for emphasis. Dr. Scrye raised his eyebrows. "You did something like ninety-eight-point-nine-nine percent of the work. We just sort of cleaned up after you."

"A gross exaggeration," she told Scrye.

"Don't you *dare* belittle your efforts toward the greatest medical breakthrough of the decade to save our jobs," Jessica snapped.

"Yikes, y'all need to take a chill pill," Scrye said, holding his hands up, palm out, in a gesture that soothed no one. "First of all, I'm ninety-eight-point-nine-nine percent sure that nobody in this room is out of a job. I mean, I gotta meet with Dr. Foster on some stuff, but I'm sure we'll figure everything out."

The team looked at Scrye, then at Thea, who could hardly contain her irritation. Not only did she loathe tedious meetings, their new boss had as much as told her that she'd need to agree to whatever he wished if she wanted to keep her team.

And the hell of it was, she would.

Chapter Two

James followed Thea Foster to her office. He was nervous as hell, and hoped to cover it up with the usual Hyper Boy Genius Bullshit.

He'd known what Thea looked like, of course; he'd memorized her personnel file and seen her employee ID photo. But the scowling bespectacled face in the picture gave no clue that Dr. Thea Foster was a stone knockout, nor did it hint at the woman's sheer presence.

Foster was tall, almost as tall as he was—at six-foot-two, Jimmy didn't run into a lot of ladies who could look him in the eye. She had the darkest, glossiest hair he'd ever seen . . . it tumbled past her shoulders, and curls escaped the headband she wore and fell across her forehead.

Her eyes were a bottomless brown, so dark they were nearly as black as her irises. So dark, when she looked at him he thought he could feel himself falling into her gaze.

Her skin was pale, like most people who spent their days in labs, but instead of the washed-out fishbelly white he expected, her skin was porcelain perfection, except for the beauty mark riding the bow of her upper lip. What they used to call the mark of a sorceress.

Like most beautiful women in a brainy trade, she dressed to hide her assets—dark brown skirt past the knee, coffee-colored blouse, dark brown blazer. Sensible flats and sensible nylons. But the gold pin on her lapel was a small Tasmanian Devil, and the frames of her glasses were purple and tipped at the ends like the old-fashioned cat's-eye glasses of the fifties.

He knew she was brilliant. He'd followed her work for years. But he'd had not the faintest clue that she was utterly, amazingly gorgeous.

It was too bad.

It made everything harder.

"Right, then," he said with forced brightness, sliding her files aside and sitting cross-legged on the edge of her desk like an overgrown pixie. She arched dark brows and slowly sat down. "Let's get to it. I know you gave PaceIC to Renee Jardin in order to fuck over your old boss."

Her eyes widened, then narrowed. He felt the temperature of the room plummet—or maybe that was just the impression he got when her eyes frosted over and her mouth hardened. "That's not true," she said quietly.

"No, really, it's fine. I mean, I admire the *shit* out of you. It was a ballsy move, no question, but now you and I have to clean up your mess, *capice?*"

"If my new employer has doubts about my past performance," she said distantly, "he is welcome to peruse the security tapes."

He threw back his head and laughed. Her eyebrows arched higher until he expected them to climb off her forehead. "Riiiiiight, Dr. Foster. You were smart enough to think up the most important find in the last hundred years, but you were too stupid to doctor the security tapes."

She reddened, and he nearly fell off the desk. Jeez, she was even prettier when she blushed—the porcelain skin took on a faint pinkish undertone, like roses in the desert. "I'll clean out my desk," she said, and rose.

He leaned forward and grabbed her wrist. For such a tall woman, her wrists were surprisingly fragile—delicately boned and not even two inches across. "Hold up there, partner. I'm not firing you. Repeat: Not. Firing. You. So don't. Get your panties. In a wad."

"My panties are none of your business." She jerked her wrist away, and he let go with a yelp before she could put him through the wall. "But if you think I'm going to stand to be insulted in my own—"

"Who's insulting you? I told you: I think what you did was hot shit. Jekell was an asshole. Who hides a cure that can help millions of people just to make a buck? Shit, the guy was already rich. How much more money did he need? You can't take it with you, right?"

"I disliked Dr. Jekell," she replied, "but I resent your insinuation."

"Oh, please." He rolled his eyes. "What, you think this is a setup? You think I'm wired? That this is an elaborate sting to get you to confess so I can fire you?" He pulled up his shirt and saw her eyes widen in alarm. "See? No wires. Want me to take my pants off, too?"

"Not unless you want to be beaten."

He was momentarily distracted by a visual of the formidable Dr. Foster in black lingerie and a riding crop. "Yow . . . look, I don't need to trick you to fire you. This is my company now. Plus, in Minnesota all employees are at-will employees: I can pink slip you if I don't like your breath. All I'm saying is I admire what you did, but the fact is, your actions cost Anodyne big bucks."

"As I said, if you doubt my word, you should terminate me."

He sighed. He'd known she would be difficult and stubborn, but he hadn't thought she'd be thick. "You know, for a genius, you're a little slow on the uptake."

"I beg your pardon?"

"We need to get to work, pronto, on something *else* you've been playing with. We need to get it perfected and into the market, and I'd like to get it to the FDA immediately. So we can't waltz around holding each other's dicks. *We have to get to work.*"

Instead of crossing her arms over her chest, like most women did when cornered, she tucked her hands into her armpits, as if the thought of holding his dick was repugnant. "I must say, you're different from most boy geniuses."

"Call me that again, and I really *will* fire you." He snorted. "It was annoying enough when I *was* a boy."

She studied him with an assessing gaze. "In many ways, you still are."

"Sticks and stones, Dr. Foster. So. Are you on board? Or what?"

"I'll be glad to get back to work," she replied quietly. "And so will my team. But what exactly do you want us to perfect?"

"Oh, didn't I tell you? I want you to invent skin. And I want you to do it in four months."

Chapter Three

He pulled up his shirt and she gasped. Supergeek he might be, but Jimmy had the upper body of a weightlifter. His abdominal muscles were sleekly defined, and his chest was lightly furred with reddish brown hair, which tapered into his shorts.

"Thea, I've wanted you from the very beginning," he whispered, crawling across her desk. "I took over this silly little biotech firm just to get closer to you."

"Really?" she gasped.

"Absolutely." His warm hands clamped over her shoulders and dragged her forward. Dimly, she heard a stack of production memos hit the floor. His kiss was bruising, astonishing in its possessiveness and—

"Dr. Foster?"

—arousing in its pure animal—

"Uh . . . Dr. Foster?"

—pure animal—

"Dr. Foster," he whispered seductively, "what the hell is the matter?"

"What?"

She blinked. She wasn't in her office, she was in her lab. Daydreaming in front of her team, who was watching her with not-quite-concealed alarm. *Blast and double blast.*

"We can take it," Jessica said bravely, fumbling with a broken Bunsen burner. She dropped it and winced. "Just tell us."

"Yeah, out with it, boss. Just stop staring at us like that. You look a little—"

"Glazed," Marshall finished.

"I beg your pardon," she said politely. "My thoughts were—" Being thoroughly overtaken by her annoying new boss. No, it would never do to say *that*. "—elsewhere. We all have jobs. In fact, we're expediting one of my back projects— Faskin."

"Artificial skin?" Jessica asked. "Hmm."

"Our new boss has given this priority resources, including funding. So let's pull all the back work and get started."

"Won't be easy," Marshall said truthfully. He tapped a high heel thoughtfully. "We shelved it because it was just about impossible to avoid host rejection."

"Yes, but I have some new ideas on that."

"That's it?" Jack interrupted. He fiddled with his rawhide choker. Thea often thought he had the look of a man who shed his lab coat for swim trunks and a surfboard the minute the workday was over. "New Guy wants us to get back to work on Faskin? You were in there kind of a long time."

"Personnel issues."

"Oh." He fiddled faster.

"No one is getting fired." *Not even me.* "He was quite— ah—adamant about that."

"Well, great!"

"Yes, great," she repeated sourly.

Chapter Four

She rapped twice and, upon hearing his exuberant, *"Entrez,* O lackey of mine!" opened the door and stepped into his office.

The Boy Wonder had certainly made some improvements in seventy-two hours. Her former boss had favored mahogany furniture, duck prints, a hidden stash of *Penthouse,* vials of cocaine, and dark carpet.

Now the office looked not unlike the toy store of the future . . . the carpet had been pulled up and replaced with dark blue tile, and there were Legos, toy robots, trucks, racetracks, giant easels, markers, chalkboards, a rainbow of chalk, and a popcorn machine.

"For heaven's sake," she said, startled.

"I know! Isn't it great?" He sighed, a great gust of relief, and tossed the red marker down beside the legal pad. It promptly rolled off the table and across the floor, where a three-inch toy robot pounced on it. "Finally, I can get some work done."

"What a thrill for us all. If you have a minute, I'd like to go over some preliminary—"

"I bet you don't think I can walk on my hands all the way across the room."

Humor him. "I'm sure you can."

"No, really. How much you want to bet?"

"Two pounds British Sterling. Now—"

He rose smoothly from behind his table—no desks in here, interestingly enough—and then bent over.

"No, really, Dr. Scrye, that's not—"

"Jimmy, or Jim. Or Scrye," he said, his voice hollow. His entire head was now beneath the table. "Heck, I answer to almost anything."

"A great relief, Dr. Scrye. Now, about these—"

"Jimmy." He walked around the edge of the table—on his hands, she observed—and his shirt pulled up, displaying that amazing chest and stomach, damn it. He hand-walked all the way over to her and stared at her legs. "Nuts. I was hoping for a skirt."

Was he really? "Ah, beneath the genius façade lurks a pig. How nice."

"Hey, after the Jackal, I'm a dream boss. Admit it."

"You're a dream boss," she parroted.

He chuckled and flipped to his feet so quickly, if she had blinked she would have missed it. His freckled face was slightly flushed from the blood rush. "So, what's up, Thea?"

"Dr. Foster."

"Aw, c'mon."

"Dr. Foster," she repeated firmly.

"Are you afraid if you're too familiar, you might fall in love with me?"

"No!"

"Ouch!" He rubbed his ear. "Jeez, you don't have to yell."

"Sorry," she said. She could feel her face getting warm. "Can we please go over this data?"

"Sure, Doc Thea." He bounded across the office and sat on the couch, which was bizarrely patterned with red ducklings against a background that matched the tile. "Have a seat." He patted the cushion beside him expectantly.

She glanced around the office, but there was nowhere else to sit except on one of the giant beanbags, and she wasn't sure her dignity would survive it.

She sat gingerly beside him. "Thank you. My team has

pulled all the back data on Faskin, and of course there's really only one problem, but so far it's been rather insurmountable."

"You can't get the artificial skin to take."

"Correct."

He was staring at her. His intense, green-eyed gaze was almost hypnotic. His eyes were the color of antique glass, the color of a perfect emerald, the—

"Can you do it? That's all I need to know."

"What?"

He snapped his fingers in front of her face, and she flinched. "Helloooooo? Can you perfect Faskin?"

"Yes," she said without hesitation. "Eventually."

"Eventually two months? Eventually sixty years? Help me out, here."

She chewed on her lower lip. "Possibly by the end of the year. I have a few ideas . . ."

"Good. Whenever you think stuff up, the world changes." He touched her hand so quickly, she wondered if she'd imagined the sensation of his skin on hers. "It's one of the coolest things about you. Sooner would be better, of course."

Her hand tingled—annoyingly—where he'd touched her. "What?"

"Thea, d'you think you can pay attention for two seconds? I said, ooner-say would be etter-bay. I want Faskin to be trial-ready by the end of the quarter."

"I'm well aware of your insanely tight timeline. What I'd like to know is why?"

"Because." He bounded up from the couch, scooped up a stack of Legos, and tossed them to her without looking. She caught it neatly in one hand and examined it. Eight inches of red, white, and blue Legos in concentric stripes. Cute. "Because because because because beeeee-*cause!* Because of the wonderful things I does!"

"Stop that."

"I've been told I have a lovely singing voice," he said, sounding hurt.

She refused to be distracted. "Why really?"

"Money, of course," he muttered, prowling around his table like a flame-haired panther. "Moneymoneymoney."

She fiddled with the Legos. "But you're already rich."

"Hey, Thea, get lost, willya? Go invent something amazing or, better yet, fix Faskin."

She slowly stood, and frowned at him. "If you don't want to tell me, that's fine, but you needn't act like such a brat."

"*You're* a brat," he snapped.

She tossed the Legos at him. He snatched the small sculpture out of the air and stared at it. "You have made a DNA helix," he observed, "out of my American Patriot Lego set."

"Simpleton," she muttered, and turned to leave.

"I know you are!" he yelled after her. "But what am I?"

Chapter Five

"Heads up," Marshall muttered. He hurried across the room, his Jelly flats clacking against the tile. "Here come the Christians. Or the lions—I forget."

Thea stifled a sigh. In an attempt to garner good publicity after the havoc the Jackal wreaked on Anodyne, PR had been arranging tours throughout the facility all week. As head of BioSecurity, she was obliged to narrate.

The head of PR, Giselle McKenzie, stuck her head through the doorway and herded Marshall away with a frantic waving motion.

"What?" Marshall said innocently. "Is my slip showing?"

"You certainly do not have to leave," Thea said coolly, withering McKenzie with a glare.

"No worries, Chief. I need to touch up my makeup, anyway." He disappeared in the area of the restrooms. Thea had no idea which one he used, even after years of working with him. She certainly wasn't going to ask.

The tour—a baker's dozen of suburbanites—followed McKenzie into the lab. As always, laymen looked disappointed at just how ordinary a working lab appeared—sort of like an industrial kitchen, except with more expensive appliances.

"This is Dr. Foster," McKenzie was babbling, "our head of

BioSecurity. Dr. Foster, maybe you could tell us what your team is working on right now?"

"Maybe," she agreed.

Silence.

"Um . . . now?" McKenzie asked, and Thea was amused to see her Adam's apple bob as she gulped.

"Certainly. Right now we're working on perfecting artificial skin."

"Like for cyborgs?" the mop-haired son of one of the suburbanites asked eagerly.

His bangs were so long she couldn't see his eyes, but she admired his stark T-shirt, black with white lettering: FUCK OFF, PUNK. *I need one of those,* she mused.

"Like in the *Terminator* and stuff?"

"Like for burn victims," she corrected patiently.

"Don't they have skin grafts for that?" another member of the group asked.

"Yes, but it's a poor technique. It takes several surgeries, and it's excruciating for the patient. Also, the risk of lethal infection is very high. With artificial skin, we could eliminate that. However, the human body is a formidable matador when it comes to fighting off invaders—in this case, artificial skin."

"A formidable what?"

She ignored the interruption. "Burns are catastrophic. And if you have burns over more than fifty percent of your body, there isn't enough healthy skin left to prevent infection or to cover the wounds. Without skin, death is inevitable.

"As recently as five years ago," she continued, "doctors would calculate a burn victim's survival rate by adding his age to the percentage of his burn. It was a heartless equation, but one that nearly always worked. Burn victims essentially die of starvation, because their strength runs out—fighting infections and such—and they waste away."

"This is fun," mop-head commented. "I'm so glad you brought me, Mom."

The woman beside him slapped his arm, but Thea smiled. "Hope endures," she said. "If we put the puzzle together—if we unlock the key to Faskin—it will make a gigantic difference. No more cadaver skin grafts—"

"You cut skin of dead bodies and put them on burn victims?" another member of the crowd—this one a young woman in her early twenties—gasped. "That is just so ewwwww!"

"We don't anymore," Thea sniffed. "It's not practical. Again, that's where Faskin comes in. After all, if a starfish can grow a new arm, and a lizard a new tail, the human body should be able to be encouraged to grow new skin."

"So Faskin isn't actually skin?"

"It's a chemical that encourages growth of the epidermis and dermis. What grows is virtually identical to your natural skin, and your body can't tell the difference. No rejection. No infection."

"So . . . it's like cloning your own skin?"

"It's like cloning the way a Big Mac is like a sirloin steak," Thea said kindly. "Very little resemblance, actually. It's technical."

"How long have you been working on Foreskin?"

"Faskin. Seven years."

"Why so long?"

"The previous management had little interest in the project," she replied. "There's very little market demand for this sort of thing. The profit potential is small. Most biotech firms are looking for the next Viagra."

A few giggles. Thea remained a stone. She thought it was utterly ridiculous that most insurance companies covered Viagra while denying coverage of birth control pills. And what a waste of time! Erections for octogenarians? With leukemia in the world? If that had been *her* lab . . .

She caught sight of Jimmy Scrye standing at the back of the room. His arms were crossed over his chest and he was dressed in knee-length denim shorts—in winter!—loafers without socks, and a dark green polo shirt. In place of a preppie alligator over his left breast, DROP DEAD was carefully stitched in red thread. No one in the tour group glanced in his direction.

They probably think he's the janitor, she thought, amused.

"To wrap things up, Faskin will change everything," she said, trying not to glance at her watch. She enjoyed educating people, but she'd declined a professorship because it would take her out of the lab too long. "And not just by lowering the death rate, although that's a very important consideration. It will also dramatically reduce scarring, reconstructive surgeries, and painful grafting. Thanks to Faskin, not only can victims of severe burns be saved, but their skin will look virtually normal."

She stopped talking and turned back to her table. The small tour group—at first startled at the abrupt end of the speech—clapped softly. She turned back around, blushing, and said nothing.

A head taller than everyone in the crowd, Jimmy smiled at her. She smiled back before she could stop herself.

Chapter Six

"Thea, darling, I've wanted you from the moment I memorized your personnel file."

"Really?"

He was crawling across the table, moving like a big, red-headed panther, knocking over burners and clipboards and charts as he came. The clatter was enormous. "Of course! Why do you think I bought this goofy little biotech firm? To get closer to you!"

"I'm relieved to hear you say that," she said, as he pounced on her and bore her to the cold tile. Interestingly, although she smacked the back of her head when they landed, it didn't hurt. "I'm afraid I'm getting a crush on you, and I'm too old for that sort of thing."

"This isn't a crush, baby," he murmured, his breath tickling her ear. "It's true lurrrrrrrrv."

"I don't think so," she said, shivering as he chewed on her earlobe. "We barely know each other."

"Never doubt it, Thea. We were made for each other. We complement each other perfectly. Also, your numbers on this are completely fucked up."

"What?"

Jimmy snapped his fingers in front of her face again. How she hated that! "My God, you must be the first Nobelqualifying scientist I've ever known who has ADD. I said, your numbers are completely fucked."

Not again! Damn it, damn it, damn it!

"I *know* that," she snapped, yanking the clipboard away from his hands. She noticed her own were shaking. She hardly ever daydreamed, and now she couldn't seem to stop. And about Jimmy Scrye, of all people! He was loud, he was annoying, he was brash, he was . . . really well built. "It's just preliminary data." She took a deep breath and forced calm. "I think the results themselves are actually quite promising."

"I agree—I guess. I mean, chemical biology is *not* my strong point. Also, you've got the handwriting of a serial killer."

"I do not!" She checked it to be sure. Was that "random fluctuation" or "ransom fatuation"?

He ran his fingers through his hair, making it stand up in all directions. She ignored the urge to smooth it back down. "Anyway, this stuff looks good, but what good is skin that disappears after a day or two?"

"It's a step in the right direction," she said stiffly.

"Sure it is. 'Hi, I'm John, it's nice to meet you . . . whoops! There goes my skin.' "

Her team, which had been carefully pretending not to listen to their conversation, muffled giggles. She glared at their backs.

"We'll do better," she said grimly, fighting the urge to hit him over the head with her clipboard.

"Hey, don't get me wrong, you guys are doing great." He braced his palms on the table and then jumped up. He crossed one ankle over his knee and she noticed again he wasn't wearing socks. "I'm just anxious to get this done."

"Why?"

"Mind your own beeswax. I wish I could help, but this isn't my field."

"You can help by staying out of the lab," she said.

He winked at her. "Ah-ah-ah! I have to keep an eye on my property."

"What is *that* supposed to mean?" she nearly yelled.

He leaned back. "Jeez, stop with the yelling! What d'you think it's supposed to mean?"

"Can we get back to work, Dr.—"

"Ah-ah-ah!"

"Jimmy," she said, her shoulders slumping in surrender.

"That'd be swell. Hey, have supper with me tonight. We'll talk about what else you need for Faskin."

"I can't," she replied, ignoring the way her heart rate jumped. "Tonight is the team potluck. Marshall is hosting."

"No, I'm not!" Marshall shouted from the other side of the room. "I have to cancel. I have—uh—"

"Mono," Jessica supplied helpfully.

"Right! I'm uber-contagious."

"We can't go, either," Jack added. "We've all got mono."

"Too much kissing during coffee breaks," Marshall said seriously.

"Super!" Jimmy said. He turned to her. "Pick you up at six?"

"All right," she sighed. Jimmy smacked her on the shoulder in a comradely way and then jumped off the table and bounded toward the elevators. She turned slowly to look at her team, who was once more deeply engrossed in their work. "Traitors."

"Thea's got a date with the boss!" Jessica squealed.

"Hush up."

Chapter Seven

Jimmy parked outside Thea's trim condo and took a deep, steadying breath. He tightened his grip on the steering wheel, then forced his fingers to loosen.

"OK," he muttered. "Be calm. It's just dinner. Just . . . mellow out, for the love of God."

Easy to say. Quite a bit harder to do. It was bad enough that his top scientist was walking around in a world-class body. Bad enough that he needed her desperately on a ridiculous number of levels . . . physically, emotionally, and practically. Worse, much worse, that she clearly didn't care for him.

There was something about her . . . As soon as she walked in the room, his mouth just ran away from him. He babbled in a constant, inane attempt to get a reaction. Any reaction. It had always been that way. Nobody had believed his IQ test results at first. He was such a goofball, the de rigeur class clown, with such poor grades the school had made him take the test three times.

Putting his strong—insane!—attraction to Thea aside, he had trouble concentrating when he allowed himself to imagine she'd perfect Faskin. God, what if she actually pulled it off? Everything could change. Everything.

The irony: He had been able to do just about anything he put his mind to, but his brain wasn't wired for biochemistry.

That is, he could do it, but not nearly so quickly or so well as Thea Foster. She was in the top ten of her field. He wouldn't have made the top three hundred. Thus, the acquisition of Doc Thea and, incidentally, Anodyne.

"Stop sitting in here thinking," he said aloud, "and get your ass up to her door."

Good advice! He opened his car door and tried to jump out, remembering too late that he hadn't unbuckled his seat belt. He'd moved so quickly, the damned thing had a stranglehold around his neck.

He wrestled with it for a few seconds and finally freed himself. Within seconds, he was ringing Thea's doorbell.

She opened the door at once. "Good evening."

She was wearing a black sheath, knee length and sleeveless, that showed off her lush figure to perfection. No stockings, and her toenails were painted dark red. Her hair was loose and flowing past her shoulders in a gorgeous dark river. She was wearing lipstick that matched her toenails, which made her complexion look even more luminous.

"Buh," he managed.

She seized him by the lapels and yanked him inside, then slammed the door.

"Wha?" he asked.

"Never mind going out," she told him. She was blinking so rapidly, he wondered if she had a nervous tic. Two dots of high color had appeared on each cheekbone. "I have ordered a pizza. I'm going to get you out of my system so I can focus at work."

"Huh?"

She kissed him so hard, his toes curled. He brought his hands up to press her closer, touching her smooth skin and marveling at the delicacy of her arms. She was so tall, such dainty limbs were a surprise.

She broke the kiss, leaving him gasping like a trout out of water, and pulled him by the tie. He followed her, shrugging out of his jacket. "So," he said cheerfully. "What kind of pizza?"

"I don't think I can do this if you talk through it," she said.

"Well, hell, don't I get a vote? What, you're just going to sexually molest me so you can get something out of your system?"

"Exactly." They were in her bedroom now. He was amused to see a giant poster of Albert Einstein, the famous picture where the elderly genius was sticking out his tongue at the camera. The double bed was a sleigh bed, the wood of the frame dark cherry; the pillows and quilt were light blue and looked exceedingly comfy. The plush gray carpet looked like it had been swept, then vacuumed twice. Interestingly, there was no dresser; instead there were neatly stacked clear plastic boxes against the far wall. She could see the clothes at a glance and get dressed fairly quickly. Efficient, and neat as a pin . . . big surprise.

He cleared his throat. "Look, Thea, I'm sorry—"

"It's all right. I have several condoms."

Several?!? "—but I need to be wooed." While he babbled, she rapidly unbuttoned his shirt. He wondered if this was some glorious dream, then dismissed the thought. If it was a dream, she'd have come to the door wearing only the lipstick. "You can't just use me and then throw me out. Oh, who am I kidding, of course you can. But you have to admit, this is very weird."

His belt was unbuckled, whipped free of the loops, and went flying across the room. Then her hands were on his zipper. "I didn't think you even liked me!" he exclaimed. He grabbed her wrists. "Do I get to undress you now?"

"Only if you don't talk," she said firmly.

He mimed locking his lips and throwing the key over his shoulder. Then he put his hands on her shoulders, gently turned her around, and unzipped her dress. He noticed with pure joy that she wasn't wearing a bra.

The dress puddled around her ankles and she stepped out of it, then kicked it in the direction of the hamper in the far corner.

She slowly turned around.

He knew he was staring at her like a lack-witted virgin, but he couldn't help it. She was just so . . . luminous and perfect. Her breasts were small and cream-colored, her nipples the color of not-quite-ripe strawberries. Her waist was also small, but her legs were amazingly long. Nude, she was all creamy skin and long legs and flowing dark hair and great dark eyes. It was like gazing upon a wood goddess, a woman whose beauty was so terrible, it might kill you.

"Should I get dressed?" she asked quietly, standing before him with her hands at her sides.

"Don't you dare."

She smiled for the first time that night. "Your pants are falling down."

"Small wonder. You tore off my belt. Well, shoot, I don't think you should be the only naked one in the room."

"A good rule of thumb," she said gravely, and then laughed.

He nearly fell; he'd been standing on one leg and pulling his socks off. "God, what a great laugh. You should do that all the time."

"I'll keep it in mind. You have one black sock and one navy sock."

"Well, I didn't think you'd notice," he whined. "Who could have predicted a dinner date where we'd be naked in sixty seconds?" He shucked off his pants and turned to put them on one of her dresser-cube things, when he heard her draw a short, surprised breath, almost a gasp.

Shit.

He didn't turn back around; he didn't want her to see he was blushing with embarrassment. Just for a minute, he'd forgotten . . .

Jimmy took a ridiculously long time arranging his pants and socks, and didn't bother slipping off his shorts. He was pretty sure she'd be telling him to get dressed any second now.

He hadn't heard her move—those bare feet in that deep carpet were wicked quiet—but started in surprise as he felt her soft touch.

"What happened?" she asked in a voice that was only curious, not pitying. "These are burns. Quite a lot of them, in fact."

"House fire," he replied shortly. "I jumped on my little sister to put *her* fire out, and a couple of burning roof tiles fell on me."

"Why didn't you tell me? I would have—perhaps you wouldn't have seemed quite such a—"

"Gaping pain in your ass?" She was still touching his burns, going from one to the other, exploring, wondering, so he kept his back to her. "It wasn't any of your business."

She turned him around and kissed him on the chin. "It isn't now, either. Come to bed."

"Right. I'll be out of here in just a second."

She took his hands and stepped backward. "You're not listening. Come to bed."

"Uh . . ."

"Jimmy Scrye, Boy Genius, not quite tracking tonight." She made an impatient sound. "Do you think I care if you have a few scars? Everyone does. You just carry yours on the outside."

"Stop it," he said. "I'm getting misty."

Chapter Eight

Thea was on her knees, gripping the headboard with her hands, and she had time to think, *Good Lord, I'm robbing the cradle. He's four years younger than I am,* and then she felt his mouth on her, trailing kisses down her spine.

His hands were big and strong and warm, and they cupped and caressed and fondled with a young man's pure enthusiasm. He hummed as he touched, a jaunty tune, and she grinned, she couldn't help it. He was just so happy to be here, with her, nude in the dark, exploring her. He made no effort to hide it.

She said, "I suppose you think that because you're the boss, you get to do all the work?"

"Actually, I was thinking the HR department might want to have a word with me after tonight."

She laughed, then gasped as he kneaded the soft white globes of her buttocks.

"God, you have the *greatest* ass. Why do you hide it beneath those awful suits?"

"Because when I go to work bottomless, the team gets distracted."

"I'll bet! Remind me to put out a new memo."

"Heh-heh. You said put out." She chortled this in a nasally deep voice, her flawless Butthead impersonation. Only one person on her team knew she could do it. Two, if she considered Jimmy on her team. After tonight, she had better.

"Thea Foster! You're just brimming with talent." He was laughing against the backs of her thighs. It tickled, but it also made her ache in an odd way. "The things we find out when we get naked . . . by the way, you smell fantastic. What is that, rose oil?"

"Guilty."

"Mmmmm." She could feel him nuzzling her, and the ache intensified, forcing her to shift her weight and spread her legs a bit. Then he was licking her, long soft licks that parted her flesh, that brought a gush of wetness he must have tasted.

She felt his thumbs on her, parting her further, and then his tongue was darting and sliding and tickling, and she groaned and pushed back against his face. She looked over her shoulder and saw his lean, muscular form crouched behind her, his fingers and tongue busy, busy, and the sight of him pleasuring her was almost enough to push her over into orgasm.

He tongued her clit—

Jesus, is he part anteater?

—while he slipped a finger inside her, and she shoved against him, harder. "Do not—" She gulped a breath. "Do not stop doing that, please."

"Like I want to?" Now there were two fingers working busily inside her, getting slick, getting slippery with her arousal, and she moaned softly and rocked against him. "Oh, *God,* you're sweet, so sweet . . ."

She gasped something in reply, and gasped again when she felt his lips settle over her clit, felt his tongue jabbing right in her very center, while at the same time his fingers were busy, busy between her legs. She rocked harder, but he kept her in place, and now a third finger was slipping into her.

A final slick stroke of his tongue did it; she nearly staggered as her orgasm tore through her, as her uterus contracted in delightful sobbing spasms. Her knees gave way and he rode her gently to the bed, then surged inside her so quickly, the tops of his thighs slapped against the backs of hers.

She moaned into the pillow; this wasn't lovemaking, this was being taken. And she didn't want him to ever stop. He was pinning her to the bed with his weight, and one of his hands was on the small of her back, keeping her in place while he stroked and took and thrust. She couldn't even thrust back; she had no leverage. So she sprawled on her stomach and took him, all of him, and felt the vibrations of another orgasm take root in her belly.

He groaned into the back of her neck when her uterus contracted, when the delicious spasms radiated outward. *He can feel me coming,* she thought, and the idea held black excitement of such magnitude it was nearly unbearable.

"Thea," he husked. "You're so slick . . . so sweet . . . and I'm about done."

"Try reciting the periodic table," she suggested.

He groaned laughter. "Greedy."

She reached down, down, and cupped his scrotum in her hand, testing the heavy, warm weight. She squeezed, very very gently, savoring the texture, and he shivered, his hips jerking helplessly, and then he was done.

He rolled off her, and they dozed.

Chapter Nine

"Stop that."

"Stop what?" she replied.

"You're thinking too much. My spider sense is tingling."

"I'm paid to think too much," she pointed out.

"You're analyzing this and what it means and what we'll do about work tomorrow." He stretched, momentarily taking up the entire bed—she had to cling to the edge or she would have fallen off—and then relaxed. "But here it is: This was your idea. So you call the shots."

"Yes, I know."

About twenty minutes had passed, long enough for her to begin to recover from their amazing encounter. She'd had her share of physical love, but Jimmy was so exuberant and skilled and hungry, it had literally left her breathless.

But he was wrong. She wasn't overanalyzing what had happened. She was wondering when they could do it again. And that was very bad. She should be pondering the next cell cycle for Faskin, not thinking about getting the mouthwash out of the bathroom and showing Dr. Scrye a very interesting chemical reaction.

Aren't you entitled to a personal life?

Well, no.

No, not at all. Too many people were depending on her. Every burn victim in the world was depending on her, not to mention countless future victims. Just like every person with heart trouble had depended on her for PaceIC.

Don't be a martyr, you silly cow.

She would if she pleased, thank you very much. She could succeed only under immense pressure. And who knew more about her pressure points than she herself?

"Uh, Thea? D'you think I could horn in on whatever conversation you're having with yourself?"

"No, it's private," she replied solemnly, and then laughed.

"Do Butthead again."

"Heh-heh. I said private."

He put his hands on his stomach and chortled, actually kicking his feet in glee. "God, that is the *best!* I wouldn't have guessed you could do that—I wouldn't have guessed you even knew who Butthead *was.*"

"I get MTV."

"I wouldn't have guessed you watched it!"

"Well," she said comfortably, rolling over and resting her chin on his stomach. "I guess we aren't so terribly smart, are we?"

"Hey, it works out," he replied, running his fingers through her thick dark strands. "You're the smartest person in this bed—by sixteen whole IQ points, I looked it up—and I'm the richest."

"Synergy has been achieved," she said dryly. "About work . . . I would prefer if we kept this between us."

"And I agree, on the condition that we have another date tomorrow night."

"Now who's greedy?" She arched her neck; his strong fingers moving through her hair felt marvelous.

"Guilty," he said, and pulled her up for a deep, sweet kiss.

Thea was pleasantly sore the next morning. It had been an extraordinary night. The man could do things with soap on a rope that were unbelievable. And they never had gotten around to ordering pizza.

She sailed past all the security measures and practically jumped off the elevator into the lab. She had several ideas about the new cell cycle and meant to get to work on them immediately.

Thea forced herself to slow. Was this her normal eagerness to start a new day in the lab, or something more? Did she have renewed urgency about Faskin so she could fix Jimmy's scars?

She thought about it all that morning, and finally decided her sin was pride, not squeamishness. His scars hadn't bothered her—she had seen much, much worse since tackling Faskin. But the fact that they bothered him *did* bother her. He had been prepared to leave last night. Had actually assumed she would throw him out after seeing the scars. Ludicrous!

No, Thea didn't want to fix them for her. But she surely did like the idea of fixing them and pleasing Jimmy. Intellectual pride . . . and the satisfaction of a job well done.

She got to work.

Chapter Ten

"How'd last night go?" Jessica asked. They were dictating notes for the team secretary to transcribe the next morning, and it was getting late. "Did you have fun?"

Indeed, and I came screaming, too.

"It was all right."

"Is he as big a goofball in a social setting?"

Yes, and he has a tremendous cock. Simply huge, and when he shoves it hurts just right.

"I suppose."

"You should see him again," she announced. Thea had always found the young scientist absurdly protective. "You guys complement each other. You're ice, he's fire. You're designer shoes, he's flip-flops. You're—"

"—vegetables and he's fruit, yes, I see the pattern you're subtly drawing, thank you. As a matter of fact, we are getting together again tonight. We came to several satisfactory conclusions last night, and are interested in achieving more."

Just then, Jimmy poked his head into the room. "Hi, Jess. Hi, Dr. Foster. You ready to go?"

"Another twenty minutes, please."

"Sure. I'll see you then. Bye. Bye, Jess."

Thea hid her relief. She'd been half afraid he'd come to

work wearing an I BAGGED DOC THEA T-shirt. Instead, he'd been the soul of discretion.

"Let's finish here," she said to Jessica, who was staring at her with eyes gone huge.

"You fucked him, didn't you?"

"Jessica!"

"Oh my God, you *did!* I can't believe it! What was it like? Did he crack jokes the whole time? He did, didn't he?"

Thea hid her eyes with her hands. "What are you, a witch?"

"Oh, come on," she scoffed. "He drives you nuts from day one, comes by the lab just to bug you, but today he's all polite and nice and just as respectful as you please. You might as well have written it on the back of your lab coat."

"Don't tell anyone," she begged.

"I won't if you won't." Jessica smiled so widely her eyes went to half-mast. "Good for you, boss. I mean it. You deserve some personal success, too, you know."

"We'll see," she said, but she certainly had a lot to think about. More so than usual, even.

"Dr. Foster, I had to restrain myself from jumping your delectable bones all damn day."

"I'm relieved you managed."

"So should we strip, or have something to eat first?"

She tossed her car keys on the hall table, put a hand on his shoulder, leaned in, and murmured in his ear, "Can't we do both?"

Jimmy fell to his knees, right there in the hallway. He clasped his hands and looked up at the ceiling. "Lord, thank you for this woman. This incredibly sexy woman. This goddess in spectacles. I owe you *huge.*"

"Get up, you look silly," she scolded, but inwardly, she was pleased. She'd never heard a man thank the Almighty for her before. "Come along, then. What do you want to eat?"

"Ummm . . ."

"Besides me," she added.

"Well, if I have to wait, then I guess I'll settle for pasta. Where's your kitchen? I never got around to seeing it last night . . ."

"You saw plenty last night; don't imply I was a poor hostess." He followed her down the hall. "I haven't been grocery shopping in a while—"

"Leave it to me. I'm used to whipping up a seven course meal out of Spagettios and Ritz crackers."

"Yech!"

He'd brought wine, which she deftly opened and poured. Then she sat on a stool by the counter and watched him work. He rooted through her cupboards and fridge, and pulled out a box of fusilli pasta, a stick of butter, a can of tuna, and salt and pepper. Within ten minutes she was eating hot, buttery pasta flavored with the ocean tang of Chicken of the Sea.

"Good," she said with her mouth full, not quite hiding her surprise.

"I'm a man of many talents," he bragged, sitting across from her with his brimming bowl. "When I'm not seducing employees, I'm whipping up gourmet pasta with substandard ingredients."

She nearly choked. "I seduced *you*, big boy. Let's keep it in mind."

"Yes, ma'am," he said humbly, and wolfed down more noodles.

"For heaven's sake. Slow down, you'll make yourself ill."

"*A.* fat chance. I have an indefatigable appetite. *B.* I forgot to eat today. And—"

She snorted. "Some genius."

"—*C.* the sooner we finish eating, the sooner I can find out if you taste as good as you smell."

She cocked an eyebrow at him and took a sip of wine. He grinned at her so good-naturedly she had to smile back. He was just so refreshingly . . . refreshing. "Did you know when you smile your eyes look even greener?"

"You should see what happens when my dick swells."

"Damn it! Now I've spit wine all over my shirt."

"So lose the shirt."

"Har-har."

"Do Butthead again," he begged.

"No." She tossed her head. "Then you'll get used to it and take me for granted."

"Never!" he exclaimed. "Do I have to get on my knees again?"

"Oh, yes. But later." She smiled at him, delighted to see he could both blush and look randy at the same time.

"Hey, I—" His voice had roughened and he cleared his throat. "Anyway, thanks for letting me come over. I'm living out of a hotel room, and it's sure nice to come to a house, y'know?"

"A hotel? Didn't you move here when you bought Anodyne?"

"Oh, hell, no. I'm just here to oversee Faskin. After that—" He mimed a bird flying away.

"Oh." *Don't be an idiot. Did you think he was in love? Did you think you were?* "I didn't realize that."

"Hey, I thought you'd be thrilled. You don't have to worry about being stuck with me once the job's done," he joked.

"Thank God for that," she said coldly, and dumped the rest of her wine down the sink. She turned on the garbage disposal and scraped the rest of the pasta—there wasn't much; they'd both been famished—down the sink. "Are you being discreet because you'll leave when you have what you need?"

"What?" he shouted over the grinding blades.

She shut the disposal off. "I said, has my kitchen met your needs?"

He blinked at the strange question. "Uh . . . sure."

"Thank you for cooking," she said formally.

"My pleasure."

"I must repay the favor."

He bowed in the direction of her bedroom. "After you."

"I mean," she said coolly, "take you out to dinner or something along those lines."

"Oh." He seemed taken aback by the abrupt temperature drop. Part of her thought that was just fine. "Sure. Anytime."

"Anytime before you leave."

"Well . . . yeah."

Genius, my large white butt. I've never known someone so smart and so dumb at the same time.

She forced a smile. "There's a special on tonight that I'd like to watch."

"Reality TV fan, eh?"

"Hardly. It's about . . ." She paused, the better to savor the man's name on her lips, in her mouth. ". . . Dr. Langer."

She sat down on the far end of the couch, and was annoyed when he plopped down right beside her. Then she was annoyed because she was annoyed. *What on earth did you expect? Marriage? For God's sake. You only jumped Jimmy to get him out of your system.*

"—went to MIT, too. My profs were in total awe of him. The couple times I met him, he seemed like a pretty good guy."

"What?"

"Jeez, did you zone off again?"

"Do *not* snap your fingers in my face, not unless you want to pull back a stump."

He raised his hands in surrender. "Whoa, easy! Guess I have to speak up in order to be heard over the voices in your head."

"Something like that," she admitted. *At least when I'm dealing with you.*

"I was just saying, when I went to MIT people were still talking about him. And he's almost twice our age."

"Almost twice *your* age," she pointed out.

He shrugged. "Like we give a shit about that."

Mollified, she picked up the remote and turned on the television. "Oooh, there he is!"

Robert Langer was explaining to the PBS interviewer that his usual methodology was to look at a problem upside down and inside out.

Thea felt her mood instantly unsnarl. "Ohhhhh," she sighed. "He's so handsome!"

"*What?* He's balding and he looks embalmed in that lighting."

"He's just so—so smart. So unbelievably smart. God, those piercing, deep brown eyes—"

"I thought you liked green eyes," Jimmy whined.

"—that big, beautiful skull . . ."

"Holding a big fat brain, no doubt."

"Oh, exactly. Exactly! Curse him for being married! You know, he's the reason I went into biomedical engineering."

Jimmy was now slumped so far down on the couch, his butt was hanging over the edge. "How fabulous."

"I could watch him forever."

"Well, this special's an hour long. For what it's worth, it'll seem like forever."

She tuned him out and listened raptly to every word uttered by the great god Langer. The hour sped by and she clicked off the TV, disappointed, when the credits rolled.

Jimmy was still slouched beside her, staring at the ceiling. "Thank Christ," he said. "That was fucking endless. I think my ass fell asleep."

"I thought you liked Dr. Langer."

"I don't like watching my best girl drool all over him," he snapped.

"Best girl?"

"Oh, be quiet." He crossed his arms over his chest and sulked.

She leaned into him and worked the first three buttons free of his shirt, then slipped her hand inside and caressed his nipple. She felt his chest heave as he took a quick breath, then his arms relaxed. "Come back to the bedroom with me?"

"Oh, this is fucking bogus! You're totally using me because that PBS special got you hot. Admit it!"

"Come back to the bedroom with me?"

"Yes," he growled. "I'll take you however I can get you."

He stood in an abrupt movement and hauled her up beside him. "If you call me Robert, I'm going home."

"Agreed." *Robert.*

When he asked her what she was laughing about, she refused to tell him.

He chased her to the bedroom.

Chapter Eleven

They helped each other off with their clothes, fumbling in their haste, and Thea noticed her bra was hanging from the curtain rod. Well, it's not like she needed that particular item of clothing anytime soon.

Jimmy, she noticed, was careful to never turn his back on her. She was torn between sympathy and amazement. She couldn't imagine the immense physical pain he'd endured, to say nothing of the trauma of the fire itself. On the other hand, he was so carefree, such an amiable clown, she was astonished he could be so self-conscious over a few scars.

She put her hands on his stomach—it was like pushing against a two-by-four—and shoved. He toppled back on the bed, clad only in one kelly green sock.

"Be right back. And for God's sake, lose the sock."

"It brings out my eyes!" he yelled after her.

She grabbed the bottle of Scope, pausing for a moment to stare at her reflection. Was this woman with mussed hair and glittering eyes really her? She was flushed with excitement and her hands were trembling. She absolutely could not wait to get her hands on Jimmy's scrumptious body. She was as giddy as a kid with her first chemistry set!

Are you going to stare at yourself, or are you going to plea-sure him out of his mind?

The latter, of course.

There isn't a single man in the world luckier than me right now. Not one.

He had a forearm thrown over his eyes; if he were to actu-ally watch Thea going down on him, he'd probably drown her.

She had sipped some mouthwash, and the next thing he knew, she was sucking his dick into her mouth. The warmth of her lips, tongue, and cheeks, coupled with the cool sting of the mouthwash, nearly made him leap off the bed.

She'd been at it for at least ten hours. Or at least that's how it felt. She wasn't shy about using her hands and fingers, either, and as a result, it felt like about three different women were in bed with him.

Thank you, Dr. Langer. I love you, Dr. Langer.

He brought his hands down and buried them in the black fire of her hair. Quite unconsciously, he dug his heels into the mattress and started to thrust against her mouth. "If you're not the swallowing type," he rasped, "it's time to let me go."

She hummed in response, which set the mouthwash to vi-brating against the tender flesh of his cock. The top of his head blew off—at least, that's how it felt—and he was gripped with spasms so fierce, he was still shuddering a minute later.

"Good heavens," Thea remarked, propping herself up on an elbow to study him. "Are you all right?"

"Holy shit," he groaned. "You're not even out of breath!"

"I lettered in swimming in college," she said primly.

"Holy God."

"It's just a chemical reaction," she teased. "We see them every day in the lab."

"Not in my lab!"

She leaned over him, pulled open the bedside drawer, and rummaged around.

"What the hell is *that?*"

"This? What does it look like?"

"That vibrator," he said, shocked, "is as long as my forearm."

She gave him an irritated glance, shoved Mr. Shaky further back into the drawer, and fished out a new box of condoms. "I don't have a steady boyfriend," she explained. "And I spend most of my time in the lab. What do you suggest? Porn mags and bubble gum?"

"First of all, you just raised the worst mental image ever. Second—" He was distracted by the box she fished out of the drawer. "Magnum extra large? My ego is getting so big, there won't be room for the two of us in this bed."

"I broke two condoms on you last night," she complained. "Thank God the third one held. I'd just as soon not have another latex wrestling match."

He laughed and Thea grinned back. She opened the box, and he said, "Uh, Thea, you're gonna have to give me a minute, here. Unlike your toy, you can't just plug me in and expect instant service."

She shrugged. "All right."

She put the box on the bedside table and sat cross-legged beside him. A moment of silence passed, broken by the tap-tap-tap of the foil packet on her thumbnails.

"Jeez, why don't you whip out a stopwatch?" he complained.

"I can see the clock from here," she pointed out, then giggled. "Sorry. You must think I'm an awful slut. Can I help it if I want my turn?"

"You'll get your turn," he growled, and pounced, burying his head between her sweet-smelling thighs.

She was wet and hot and salty-sweet, and she made the most delightful noises in the back of her throat as he worked her with his tongue and lips and fingers. He felt her fingers trailing through his hair, cupping his neck, drifting down—

Oh my God!

He jerked back. "That's enough," he said roughly.

"Wh-what?" Her breasts were heaving and she put a hand up to brush her bangs out of her eyes. "What's the matter?"

He snatched the condom out of her hand, fumbled it out of the packet, and rolled it onto his thick erection.

"Talk about leaving a girl out in the cold," she said, trying to tease, but her eyes were large with worry.

"Just didn't want to wait anymore, is all." He grabbed her, flipped her over, pulled her legs apart, and drove into her. Her gasp was almost buried under his groan. He could see the white globes of her gorgeous butt working, rising to meet him, and he kept his hands on her outer thighs, keeping her spread for him. Oh, it was glorious, it was like fucking wet silk, she was—

She was gone! She had put her hands on the floor and crawled away from him with a sharp jerk. His dick waved indignantly.

"What the *hell?*"

She rolled over, glaring at him from the floor. "You only take me from behind. We're never made love face to face. It's because of your back, isn't it? You're worried about the scars."

"Get back up here," he said calmly. "Right now."

"I decline. You're a user, Jimmy. Spectacular between the sheets, but a user." She was standing up, looming over him in naked glory. In the gloom her skin looked like marble; he was facing an enraged goddess: Athena. "You're using me to get your Faskin, you aren't staying around once you have what you want, and Doc Thea's good enough to fuck as long as you're not face to face. *God forbid* we actually look in each other's eyes."

She's right.

She's wrong!

His intellect warred with emotion; emotion won. "You're so full of shit. You had absolutely no life before I came along. I jazz things up and you know it."

"If I wanted jazz, I'd buy a Louie Armstrong record," she snapped, and despite himself, he had to bite his lip to hide the grin. "Don't flatter yourself, Dr. Doofus. My life doesn't need fixing. Yours does. Do you think if I touch one of your scars, I'll turn to stone? Throw you out? Never let you touch me again?"

"Jesus, *shut up!* Are we going to finish this or are you going to play amateur shrink?"

"Amateur shrink, seeing as how you've finally given me a choice about something. Your scars are no big deal. They wouldn't matter to me if they were all over your face."

He stepped off the bed and seized her by the shoulders. "You don't know what the fuck you're talking about," he snarled. "Pray you never find out."

He thrust her away from him. He didn't dare touch her again. His hands wanted to fly up and slap the shit out of her. Wanted to yank her hair and make her scream and stop that talk about scarred faces being no big deal. He cast about frantically for his pants, terrified he would hurt her before he could escape.

Suddenly, the world was whirling denim as his Levi's smacked him in the face. "Don't let the door hit you in the gluteus maximus on the way out," she said. She spun him around, braced her hands—

His inner child, the voice of the ten-year-old he'd once been, screamed. *She's touching my back! Don't, it'll hurt, stop hurting me!*

—and shoved. Good thing the bedroom door was open, or he would have broken his nose.

"Tomorrow's going to be a fun day at the office," he said angrily.

"I quit!"

The bedroom door slammed in his face. He stepped into his jeans—thank God his keys were still in the pockets—and debated whether to go after his shirt and socks.

He heard a *whump!* and guessed she'd thrown herself on the bed. Muffled sobs drifted out into the hallway. He leaned his head on the door for a good minute, listening, but didn't dare go in. His hands might get away from him. Bad enough his mouth already had.

He turned around and left. It had started to rain, which was just as well, because he wouldn't have to wonder if raindrops were running down his face, or something else.

Chapter Twelve

He pulled her to him and cuddled her against his side. His hand slipped down and cupped one of her breasts, gently testing the weight. "Thea, darling, I wanted you the moment I laid eyes on you. As the guy in the Gillette commercials said, 'I liked you so much, I bought the company!'"

She sighed as his thumb rubbed across her nipple, coaxing it to stiffness. "Really?"

"Of course, really." He leaned down and brushed her lips with his. "Did you ever doubt it?"

"Frankly, yes."

"Dr. Foster!"

"What?"

"I didn't say anything," Jimmy said with a contented sigh. "Let's play hooky and have sex all day.

"Dr. Foster!"

"I'd—I'd love to. I think we already did. Look how low the sun is."

He dropped a kiss to her temple, then shrieked in her face, *"Open the door right now!"*

She gasped and sat bolt upright. The sun really *was* low. She was alone, and someone—it sounded like Jessica—was pounding and kicking the door.

"IQ, if you've been killed or murdered in there, I am calling the police! So you better answer the door!"

She bolted from the bed, snatched the robe from the back of the bedroom door, shrugged into it, and raced down the hallway. She unlocked her front door and jerked it open, then had to dodge Jessica's pounding fist.

"Oh, thank God. Finally!"

"What?" she snapped.

"*What,* what? You haven't missed a day of work. Ever. Ever-ever. The team was worried about you, so I offered to check on you. Are you sick?"

"Sick of work," she said pointedly, and started to swing the door shut. Jessica jammed her foot into the gap, then shouldered her way past. Bemused, Thea let her. "Did you know your house smells like tuna?"

"He fixed supper for me." Then she slapped her hands over her eyes and cried like a child, for the first time since—well, last night.

"Jeez," Jessica said, impressed. She pushed the cup of tea closer to Thea.

"I'm sorry to burden you with my troubles."

"I don't mind that. You're the best boss I ever had; I want you to be happy."

"I'm the only boss you ever had."

"Never mind. It's just . . . I gotta say, I didn't know you *could* cry. And over that weirdo, Dr. Scrye? Bizarre!"

"I can't believe I was so stupid. I actually thought he liked me for me. Not because of what I could do for him. Or to him," she added bitterly, thinking of the bottle of Scope.

"Look, he probably freaked out because you were getting too close. I'm sure he adores you. God knows he was an absolute beast at the office today."

She perked up. "Really?"

Jessica raised her pinkies and linked them together in a cross. "Swear. He was a total asshole. He made Marshall cry!

Told him he couldn't pull off the purple pantsuit because it was a fall color."

Thea slammed her fist on the table. "Bastard," she hissed.

"Right. Anyway. I'm glad you're OK. Relatively speaking. Um . . . there's a rumor . . . I'm sure it's not true, but the team made me promise to—"

"Yes, I resigned. I'm very sorry, but I cannot work for that man another day. Another minute."

"Well, will you let us know where you get work? And if you'll be budgeted for a team?"

"You don't need to leave on my account," she protested. "Anodyne will be in the black again soon. There's plenty of work left."

"We'd rather work with you. It's like . . ." Jessica's eyes went faraway. "Like you make us more than we are. Like you're so smart, you've got brains to spare for the rest of us. And as a result we work better. We *are* better."

"I wasn't especially smart last night," she commented, but she was pleased. Jessica was quite wrong, of course—her team had six PhDs and three MDs between them—but it was nice of her to say. "In fact, I'd better get this over with."

"I'll go—"

"You will not go with me. I don't need an escort. Although," she added dryly, "security will likely be escorting me out."

"Well. If you're sure."

"I am. Thank you for checking on me. I'm sorry I tried to close the door on your foot."

Jessica laughed. "I have two. So it's all right."

She had boxed up her files—those she could legally take with her—and cleaned out her desk. Now she printed out her formal resignation and fantasized briefly about stapling it to Jimmy's forehead.

It was after ten . . . she'd slip it under his door and be on her way. And never, never think of Anodyne or Faskin or Jimmy Scrye again.

His office door was open a crack and light was spilling out into the hallway. She hoped that meant he'd simply left it unlocked. She couldn't hear anyone speaking, so she simply pushed the door open with her tented fingers.

Jimmy was standing beside a Lego Eiffel Tower as tall as his hip, hugging a woman. From the back, she had the same flaming red hair, and it bounced around her shoulders like a mobile sunset. Thea was shocked at how the sight was like a knife between her shoulder blades.

Jimmy's eyes, which were closed as he blissfully hugged the whore, flew open. "Thea! Jeez, are you all right? I mean—uh—"

She flapped the piece of paper at him. "I came in to pack. Here is my formal resignation. I regret I am unable to give you proper notice."

The hussy started to turn. Jimmy started to talk faster. "Thea, please don't. I—the company needs you. We can't finish without you."

"You'll have to."

The slut pulled away and faced Thea, who nearly dropped her resignation. The left side of her face was mostly flawless . . . cream-colored skin, a gorgeous sprinkling of freckles, cheekbones you could cut yourself on. Sparkling green eyes. The right side . . . a ruin. Thea was looking at long-healed skin grafts.

"Hi," the very nice woman said. "I'm Patrice, Jimmy's twin sister."

Your scars are no big deal.

"I'm Dr. Foster," Thea said. "It's nice to meet you."

They wouldn't matter to me if they were all over your face.

"It's nice to meet *you*. You're all Jimmy talks about."

Oh, dear God. How blind she'd been. How unforgivably stupid.

"Thank you."

She thought back to what the team had told her on his first day. Orphaned at sixteen via a house fire, that's what they said. An MD who started his first biofirm at twenty-two.

I jumped on my little sister to put her fire out, and a couple of burning roof tiles fell on me.

A scarred man who made a practice of rescuing ailing biotech firms and turning them around.

Why? For Patrice. All for her. It had nothing to do with *his* scars. Oh, she was an idiot.

"—came to check out Jimmy's new digs," Patrice was saying. "He told me you were going to help him put me out of business." She said it in a tone of perfect good cheer.

"Um . . . Miss Scrye . . ."

"Dr. Scrye-Drie."

"Scrye-Dry?"

"I hyphenated my name when I got married."

"Thereby giving herself the dumbest name ever," Jimmy said, rolling his eyes.

"Shut up," Patrice said, giving him a pinch. "What were you saying, Thea?"

"Ah . . . well, Faskin offers great promise. But it can't—that is to say, we can't use it to—um—"

"Fix my horror of a face?" Patrice Scrye-Drie laughed. Laughed! "Of course not. Faskin will only work on fresh burns, correct?"

"Yes. Maybe someday . . ."

"Right. Well, that's good enough for me. That's all I ever wanted. I've got a husband who thinks I'm the sexiest thing he's ever seen, but I've got a sucky job."

"She's the director of the burn ward at Chicago General," Jimmy explained. "Does six grafts a day."

"Not for long," Patrice said. "Not if you finish what you started." She smiled. The right side of her face didn't move, but she had a dimple buried in her left cheek. The effect was surprisingly charming. "You will, won't you? Don't let my jerkoff of a brother chase you away."

"I'm so, so sorry about last night," Jimmy said earnestly. "I didn't mean to treat you like—"

"I don't want to discuss it." She saw him flinch, and wanted to tell him she'd been a bit of a jerkoff herself . . .

that's why she didn't want to get into it. Especially in front of Patrice.

How blithely confident she had been! What a supreme ass!

"I'll—I'll stay. Until Faskin is done. That could be six weeks or six years . . . I don't know."

Jimmy looked distinctly relieved. Patrice clapped her hands. "That's great! Thanks so much, Thea!"

"I didn't—I didn't feel right, leaving my work unfinished anyway," she said awkwardly.

"Put me out of business, Thea. You promise me, now."

"I promise."

They smiled at each other, like sisters.

Chapter Thirteen

"C'mon, IQ. Pack it up for the day."

"Quit it," Thea said, her gaze riveted on the chemical reaction before her.

"Come *on!* You've got to get out of here. You haven't left the lab in four days."

"Hmm . . ."

"You're going to kill yourself for that redheaded weirdo."

Which one? "Most likely."

"Dr. Foster, please!"

"Good-bye."

Jessica huffed out. She'd been the last team member to stay. It was midnight . . . at least, it had been the last time she checked her watch. Her stomach, which had been growling constantly, had finally quit.

Good. She didn't have time to eat.

She was inches away. She felt it. She *smelled* it! It had been like this with PaceIC, too . . . years of frustration, followed by unconscious insight, followed by success. While she'd been sulking and sobbing and sleeping in bed, pieces fell together in her brain and the answer, which had eluded her for so long, was inches away.

She would get this done. She would keep her promise. She would make it up to Jimmy. She would . . .

... would ...

Why was it getting so dark?

"Oh, Christ. Thea!" Hands on her shoulders, shaking. Light taps on her cheeks. Somebody yanked her glasses off. Firm fingers at her throat, checking her pulse. A thumb peeled her eyelid up. "Thea! Shit, where's that fucking cell phone—"

"You keep it in an ankle holster like a complete yutz," she said, batting his hand away from her eyes. "Remember?"

Jimmy was staring down at her. He was pale, and his green eyes burned like lamps. He was holding her glasses protectively curled in his hand like a baby bird. His fingers moved to her throat again, to check her heart rate. "It's three o'clock in the morning, you dumbass! Killing yourself won't help my sister."

She snorted irritably. "I've worked longer than this without sleeping or eating."

"*Eating?*"

"Stop yelling. Help me up."

"The hell. I'm calling an ambulance."

"Just help me up," she repeated tiredly. "You're an MD, you know perfectly well I don't need to go to the hospital. Besides, thanks to the HMOs, I could have end-stage cancer and they wouldn't admit me."

He sat on his heels and thought about it. "Promise to rest."

"... for a while."

"OK. Oooooooof!" He strained and lifted her.

"Don't be overdramatic. I can walk."

"You weigh a ton."

"Thank goodness I haven't eaten, then."

He laughed and nearly dropped her. He staggered through BioSecurity and brought her to the executive conference room. The sight of it made her giggle.

"What's funny, honey?"

"Oh, I caught an employee having sex in here once. I mean, they had just finished, but you could tell what they'd been up to. I thought it was monumentally stupid of them at the time. I didn't know . . ."

"What?" he said, placing her on the couch behind the table.

"Never mind."

"Do not move from that couch. Not unless you want your ass kicked."

She yawned. "Oh, I wouldn't want that."

He backed out of the room, and then she heard him running down the hall to his office. He was back a minute later. "Drink up," he said, popping the top and handing her the Coke. The can felt ice cold and she pressed it to her cheek. "That'll get your blood sugar up."

She emptied the can in seven noisy gulps, then laid back and belched lightly. "Oh, that's better."

"You are *so* sexy when you're gassy."

"Shut up. I'm not speaking to you." She flushed, embarrassed. "Also, you shouldn't be speaking to me."

"Forget it." He sat down cross-legged beside the couch. It was so low, he still loomed over her. "You couldn't have known. I should have told you. I just—it's a private thing."

"I understand," she said fervently. "Believe me."

"No, you were the one person in the world I *should* have told," he said, serious for once. "But old habits, you know."

"I shouldn't have been so smugly judgmental."

"And I shouldn't have been a raving sociopath. Well, we've both beaten our breasts pretty well, haven't we?"

"You leave my breasts out of this."

He laughed, leaned over, and pressed a soft kiss to her mouth. "Sleep," he said.

She did.

A minute later, she opened her eyes to blazing sunlight. The shades hadn't been drawn, and she could see it was almost noon.

"Wow!" she said.

"What? What?" Jimmy sat up beside the couch, blinking dazedly. His hair was standing wildly in all directions. He had carpet marks on his left cheek. "Are you all right? What's wrong? I'll call the—"

"Sorry." She smiled and touched his cheek, smoothing out the checkerboard pattern. "It just surprised me . . . It felt like I was sleeping only a few minutes, but a good nine hours have gone by. Also, I could play tic-tac-toe on your face."

"I always knew you were a kinky bim."

"Did you really sleep on the floor all night?"

"Yeah." He ran his fingers through his hair, which made it stand up just as wildly . . . but in the opposite direction. "You were my patient."

"Oh, you spend the night with all your patients?"

"Just the ones who drive me batshit. Stay here."

"Good doggy," she muttered as he stumbled out.

She did not obey. She got up, carefully tested her legs, and was pleased when they held her weight. She used the executive washroom, shook her head in despair at her reflection, and was lying placidly on the couch when Jimmy returned.

"OK, you want Pringles, Fritos, or Nachos for breakfast? Lunch, I mean?"

"Do you have anything that doesn't end in 'os'?"

"I *said* Pringles. Also, M&M's."

She made a face. "Pringles, please."

"Just a few," he warned, popping the top and dumping a few chips into her hands. "I ordered some soup and sandwiches from the cafeteria. They'll be up in a few minutes."

"I'd rather eat my own vomit."

"Obviously you haven't eaten at the caf since I took over. The food's much better."

He was right. Her sandwich had been brushed with basil mayonnaise; the tomato soup was velvety perfection and tasted like summer. She forced herself to eat slowly. No use having it all come back up.

Jimmy gathered up the garbage as she lay back down with

a sigh. "Oh, that was good. Where is everybody? I haven't heard a soul in the hallway."

"It's Sunday," he replied, stomping the garbage until it fit in the overflowing can. "We're it, sugar. Come on, I'll take you home."

"Absolutely not." She stood. Yes, that was *much* better. "I've got to get back to work."

"Absolutely not. Thea, you'll get it. I know you will. Shit, the whole company knows."

"No pressure or anything," she muttered.

"If you don't promise to rest and not come back to work until Tuesday, I'll fire your ass."

"Don't be an idiot," she snapped.

"Sticks and stones, sugarplum."

"You can't fire me. Your sister is depending on you."

"Watch me, gorgeous." He crossed swiftly to her and held her hands in his. "It's not worth your health."

"Jimmy, you don't understand. Let me work," she pleaded. "I'm so close! I know I'll—"

He kissed her. She knew she should finish the argument, but the pressure of his lips on hers was, in its way, a compelling argument on its own. She looped her arms around his neck and licked his lower lip.

"Ummmm. I've missed you."

"Gorgeous?" she teased. "Are you farsighted? I'm a wreck."

"Gorgeous," he repeated firmly. "And—uh—I'll take you home."

"What's wrong?"

"Nothing. I mean, I have this gigantic hard-on right now—"

"Gigantic, hmm?"

"But you're in no shape to—"

"If you won't let me work," she said, slipping her fingers into his jeans and feeling the throbbing warmth he had for her, "you'd best let me play doctor, Doctor."

He closed his eyes and squeezed her so hard she squeaked. "Um. You. Uh. Shouldn't do that. Um. Don't stop."

She unzipped his fly, reached around, and squeezed his ass. Oh, lovely. The flesh barely gave way. "You are in *great* shape," she commented. "But you devour a constant stream of junk food and I've never seen you exercise."

He leered. "Sure you have."

"Oh. Pervert."

"OK," he said suddenly, pushing her toward the couch. "But you have to let me do all the work."

"Phooey, that's no fun."

"I mean it, Thea."

"You'd appear more stern if you weren't yanking off your jeans as fast as you could."

"When we're done, I plan on strangling you," he said, exasperated.

"When we're done, you won't have any strength left."

She got off the couch and crawled beneath the conference table. "Here," she said, patting the carpet beside her. "I want to do it here. Also, I owe Renee Jardin an apology."

"Who?" He crawled next to her.

"Never mind."

They undressed each other, growing more and more urgent, and once Jimmy sat up too quickly and banged his head on the underside of the table. This sent Thea into gales of laughter and she scarcely noticed when her skirt went flying over his shoulder.

He buried his face in her cleavage, licking and nibbling and sucking, and she could hear her breath shortening. "How do you feel about kids?" he asked, his mouth muffled against his flesh.

"What?"

"Kids. Ankle-biters. Nose-miners. Rugrats."

"Thanks for translating." He lightly nipped the sensitive swell of her breast and she shivered. "I always figured I'd artificially inseminate myself. Twice."

"Uh-huh. Well, how about the old-fashioned way?"

"That would be all right in a pinch," she said, picturing

herself swelling with Jimmy's child, a red-haired beauty with her eyes and his sense of irreverence.

"OK, good, we're agreed on that. How do you feel about getting married?" He reached down, gently parted her, and slipped a finger inside. He found her ready . . . more than ready.

She raised her knees and spread herself before him. He made a soft sound in his throat, a purr of pleasure.

"It would depend," she said breathlessly, moving against his hand, "on whom I asked."

He raised himself up on his elbows and smoothed her hair away from his face. "If you asked me?"

She reached down and clasped his throbbing, velvety length. "Then I would love marriage."

"So. Ask me."

"Right now?"

"Well, it's possible I'm about to knock you up. So I should make an honest woman out of you." He pulled up her legs and entered her with excruciating slowness. She locked her ankles behind his back.

"Ask me," he breathed in her ear.

"It's crazy," she gasped.

He pumped harder, lengthening his strokes, and she groaned and met him, thrust for thrust.

"Ask me."

"Will—you—marry—me??"

"Yes."

He slowed his strokes, looking down to watch himself entering her again and again. "It's still crazy," she groaned, as he moved against her, within her. Slowly. Sweetly. "We've only known each other three weeks."

"Three weeks and two days," he corrected her, panting slightly. He stopped moving, resting within her.

"Oh, now you're just being mean," she joked.

"I want to say this while I can sort of think. I mean, most of the blood in my brain headed south a while ago."

"Men," she sighed, shaking her head.

"And I don't care about how long it's been," he added gently. "I care about you. I love you. I loved you the minute I saw you on the news about PaceIC."

"You saw me?"

"Couldn't take my eyes off you. Something about your face—you looked proud, but you looked a little scared with all those microphones in your face. Of course, the cameras didn't do you justice, because in person you were—wow."

He was still throbbing within her, which was delightfully distracting. She squirmed, but he didn't budge. "That's . . . ummm . . . a lovely thing to say. I couldn't *stand* you the moment I saw you."

He laughed, a low rumble against her chest. "Why do you think I bought this company?"

"Wh-what?"

"Anodyne. I bought it because—well, because I wanted you to finish Faskin, but also because I wanted to get to know you. I wanted you my first day here."

"Oh, no!"

"What?"

"Oh, shit!"

"Jeez, am I hurting you? What's wrong?"

"I'm dreaming!" she wailed. "This is all a dream, the best one I ever had. Any minute now you're going to turn into Jessica."

He pinched her nipple. She yelped. "Satisfied?"

"Well . . . that did hurt a little. Maybe it's not a dream. God, I hope not," she added fervently.

"Also, babe, we gotta talk . . . You dream about me and then I turn into Jessica?"

"Just shut up and fuck me before I wake up."

He'd been bending down to kiss her, and laughed in her mouth. "Yes, ma'am. It's just as well. If I have to stay still any longer, my balls will blow up."

"You say the nicest things—ah!"

He thrust, and she pressed her heels against his back, forcing him deeper. She clutched his shoulders and shoved back at him. She could hear how wet she was. How wet he'd made her.

"Put your arms around me," he murmured. "I want to feel as much of you as I can."

She did, clutching his back, feeling his muscles work as he fucked her, pleasured them both. She was staring into his emerald eyes when her orgasm raced through her.

"Ahhhh, Christ!" he groaned. "Anybody tell you—when you come—all your muscles lock?"

"Well," she said breathlessly, "it's physiologically . . ."

"No, *all* your muscles."

"Oh." She giggled. "No. Nobody's ever noticed, I guess. Plus, my vibrator's not the chatty type."

"Do not talk about Mr. Shaky," he growled.

"Oh, I think Mr. Shaky might be due for early retirement." She tightened her grip and thrust her tongue in his ear. He jerked in response, then stiffened and shuddered all over.

"I love you," he said.

She tried to smooth his hair, but it was a lost cause; it kept springing up between her fingers. "I love you, too. But it's still crazy."

"Ask me if I give a fuck."

She jabbed him. "Nice!"

He jabbed her back. Things degenerated into the first tickle fight of her adult life.

Epilogue

From *People* magazine.
The World's Most Beautiful People Issue, March 25, 2005

Exotic, stunning, and with the carriage of a queen, Dr. Thea Scrye is much more than just a pretty face. A contender for the Nobel Prize for Medicine, Foster gave hope to countless burn victims when she perfected Faskin, a phenomenal advance in artificial skin.

"She's a genius," Dr. Patrice Scrye-Drie, former director of the Chicago General Burn Unit, says enthusiastically. "She put me out of a job. Our whole family just loves her to death. She's just what my brother needed. Have you talked to them? Did you see my niece? Seven months old and already talking! I have pictures. I have a lot of pictures."

Scrye-Drie, Thea Scrye's sister-in-law, credits her brother's efforts with moving Faskin toward completion. "Jekell had no interest in it. But Jimmy revived the project and gave Thea everything she needed."

Dr. James Scrye, hotshot rescuer of ailing biotech

firms, gives all the credit to his wife, who in turn takes it. Interestingly, the Scrye family boasts several brilliant physicians. In an extended family totaling over thirty members, only two are not in the medical field.

Although it has wrought great good, Faskin came into being from tragedy. The Scrye twins lost their parents in a house fire when they were still children, and have been seeking an alternative to the trauma of skin grafts ever since. Both were injured in the fire that killed their parents.

When asked about his bride, Dr. Jimmy, as he insists on being called, replied, "She's a goddess. Write that down. Two 'd's. Goddess."

Dr. Thea Scrye, who has suffered much media attention due to her extraordinary breakthrough, was not inclined to share much with People. "You have a Most Beautiful issue? For real? I thought my husband was playing a joke. How exquisitely stupid. Go to a hospital. Donate blood."

Smitten by the wedding photo her husband gleefully faxed, this reporter complied.

We don't think you will want to miss
HE SEES YOU WHEN YOU'RE SLEEPING
by Lori Foster, a novella in JINGLE BELL ROCK.
This Brava October 2003 anthology also features
Janelle Denison, Susan Donovan, Donna Kauffman,
Alison Kent, and Nancy Warren. Here's a sneak peek.

Frances had paused in front of her tree to straighten a plump Santa ornament. The delicate glass reflected the white twinkly lights, looking almost magical. But there'd be no magic for her this year. What she wanted most, Santa couldn't put under her tree.

After working all day, she was hot and tired, and so when What-She-Wanted-Most knocked on her door, she almost jumped out of her skin. She knew it was Booker, because she knew his knock, just as she knew his laugh, his tone of voice when he was excited, and his scent. God, she loved his scent.

With her heart swelling painfully, she opened the door with a false smile. As usual, he looked dark and sexy and so appealing, her pulse leaped at the sight of him.

Hands snug in his pockets, his flannel shirt open over a white thermal and nicely worn jeans, he leaned in her doorway. His silky black hair was still damp from a shower and his jaw was freshly shaved. He had a rakish "just won the lottery" look about him and the way he murmured, "Hi" had her blinking in surprise.

Somehow, he was different. There was a glimmer in his dark eyes, a special kind of attentiveness that hadn't been there only the day before. His gaze was direct and almost . . .

intimate. Yeah, that was it. And he wore a funny little half smile of expectation.

Expectation of *what?*

Uncertainly, Frances managed a reply. "Hey, Booker. What's up?"

He stepped inside without an invite, but then, they were *friends* and Booker visited with her a lot. Whenever he wasn't working—or with Judith—he came by to play cards, watch sports, or just shoot the bull. Like he would with a pal.

Maybe it was the holidays making her nostalgic, but when she thought of being Booker's pal for the rest of her life, she wanted to curl up and cry.

A stray lock of hair had escaped her big clip and hung near her eyes. Taking his time and stopping her heart in the process, Booker smoothed it behind her ear.

No way in hell did he do that with his guy friends. She gulped.

In a voice low and gentle and seductive, he said, "What have you been doing that has you all warm on such a cold snowy day?"

Unnerved, Frances backed up out of reach. Booker stepped close again. "I, ah . . ." She gestured behind her. "I'm moving my room."

"Yeah?" He looked at her mouth. "Want to move it next door with me?"

She shook her head at his unfamiliar, suggestive teasing. "I'm switching my bedroom with my studio because the light is better in that room now."

As an artist, she liked to take advantage of whatever natural light she could get. In summer, she used her smaller guest bedroom for sleeping so that the larger room could be filled with her canvases and paints and pottery wheel. But now with winter hard upon them, the light was different. More often than not, long shadows filled the room, so she was switching. If nothing else, it gave her a way to fill the time rather than think of Booker and Judith snuggled up in front of a warm fire, playing kissy-face and more.

Booker stepped around her and closed the door. "Maybe I can help. What else do you have to move?"

Now that was more like the Booker she knew and loved. "Just the bedroom furniture. I already moved the small stuff and my clothes." She turned to meander down the hallway and Booker followed. Closely. She could practically feel him breathing on her neck. Neil Diamond's Christmas album played softly in the background, barely drowning out the drumming of her heartbeat.

Today, even Neil hadn't been able to lift her spirits.

As they passed the kitchen, they walked beneath a sprig of mistletoe hung from a silver ribbon. Because she was a single woman without a steady date—without any date really—Frances had put it up as decoration, not for any practical use. She paid it little mind as she started under it, until Booker caught her by the upper arm.

Turning, she said, "What?"

Gently, he drew her all the way around to face him. He looked first into her eyes, letting her see the curious heat in his, then he looked at her mouth. His voice dropped. "This."

In the next instant, Frances found herself hauled up against his hard chest while his hands framed her face.

Startled, she thought, *He's going to kiss me.*

Just as quickly, she discounted that absurd notion. Booker was a friend, nothing more. He was involved with Judith. He didn't see her as a—

His mouth touched hers.

She went utterly still outside, but inside things were happening. Like her heart hitting her rib cage and her stomach fluttering and her blood taking off in a wild race through her system . . .

"Frances?" He whispered her name against her mouth.

Dazed, her eyes flickered open. "Hmm?"

Booker held her face tipped up, brushed her jaw with his thumbs, and kissed her again. It was a gentle, closed-mouth kiss, but there was nothing platonic about it. His mouth was warm, soft, moving carefully over hers. His tongue traced the seam of her lips with such enticing effect that her toes curled and her hands lifted to his hard shoulders. Booker groaned, tightened his hold—and Frances came back to her senses.

"*Booker.*" She shoved him away, suffused with indignation and hurt and an awful yearning. "What do you think you're doing?"

Because she was nearly as tall, her push had thrown him off-balance. He caught himself, grinned at her, and said, "Something I've been thinking about doing for a long time."

And we are proud to present BAD BOYS TO GO
with Lori Foster, Janelle Denison and Nancy Warren,
coming in November 2003, from Brava.
Here's a preview of Lori's story,
BRINGING UP BABY.

No two ways about it: Anabel just wasn't proper mother material. He thought of mothers as being like his own—no-nonsense, understated, ready with a hug and advice. His mother *looked* like a mother. Soft, a little rounded, casual and comfortable.

Anabel looked like . . . not a mother. He couldn't label her, but there was nothing comfortable about her. Exciting, yes. Hot, definitely. But not maternal.

Even while she'd been pouring her heart out to him, a part of his mind kept thinking how sweet it'd be to push her to her back on his desk, to tug those threadbare jeans down her hips and thighs so he could . . .

Suddenly she slid off the desk and started toward him. "I know what you're thinking, Gil."

Along with the look in her eyes, that throaty tone brought him out of his reverie. "You haven't got a clue." If she did, she sure as hell wouldn't get so close to him.

"Wanna bet?" He caught his breath when she leaned into him, her hands sliding up his chest to rest on his shoulders. Her cool fingertips brushed the heated skin of his nape. Eyes direct, even challenging, she whispered, "You're thinking about sex. With me. I've seen that look on your face before."

He didn't back down. "What look?"

Her smile curled, lighting up her eyes, flushing her cheeks. "Well, the look before you just went blank. It's this sort of heated expression, very direct and interested and naughty."

He caught her shoulders to hold her away—and instead, he just held her. His heart thundered and the muscles of his abdomen and thighs pulled tight. "You're mistaken."

"Oh really?" She went on tiptoe to brush her nose against his throat. "Mmm. You smell good, Gil."

Her breath whispered over his skin with the effect of a lick. Her breasts, shielded only by a clinging shirt, brushed his chest.

"Anabel." He meant his tone to be chastising, and instead it reeked of encouragement.

Her hand left his shoulder to glide down his chest, down, down to the waistband of his slacks where she lingered, making him nuts, causing his lungs to constrict. Her lips moved nearer to his and at close range, she stared into his eyes.

"You want me, Gil. Admit it."

He wouldn't admit a damned thing. But neither could he deny it.

The darkening of her eyes should have given him warning. But when her slender fingers drifted lower, cupping his testicles through his slacks, he was taken completely off guard. To call her brazen would be an understatement. To call him unaffected would be an outright lie.

She held him, gently squeezed, expertly stroked. "You're already hard," she whispered.

Yeah, from his ears to his toes, but did she have to sound so pleased about it?

Still in that soft whisper, she purred, "Gil, I want you, too. I always have." As she said it, she moved her fingers up to his throbbing cock, teasing his length, deliberately arousing him further, pushing him. "We would be good together. I know you, know what you like and what you want. I'll do anything, Gil. Anytime you want, any way you want."